DIAMOND ON ICE

Lacey Dancer

A KISMET® Romance

METEOR PUBLISHING CORPORATION

Bensalem, Pennsylvania

Thank you, Maureen, for your confidence
and belief in me.

All writers need that kind of faith.

LACEY DANCER

Lacey Dancer is a woman of many interests. Her husband and writing are numbers one and two; but that doesn't stop her from collecting antique salt-cellars, an assortment of farm animals, and learning organic gardening. Roses and peonies are her favorite flowers and weaving words into dreams of love the best way to earn a living.

PROLOGUE

"And now, ladies and gentlemen, for the high-light of our ice show extravaganza. Olympic Gold Medalist, three time World Figure Skating Champion, master of the silver blades, our own, the one and only, Jason 'Iceman' Starke."

The lights in the arena dimmed, plunging the standing-room-only crowd into a black velvet silence. Jason skated onto the center of the rink, mentally grimacing at the effusive introduction. In his opinion, voiced only in his mind, never aloud, the MC should have added "the brilliant techni-cian without the soul to appreciate the gift of his own skill." For one moment his lips tightened, flattening to hold back the thought that had been haunting him more frequently the last few years. With his program to do, he couldn't afford to have his concentration upset. Taking his opening posi-tion, he wondered if, for once, he would capture the elusive emotions he chased every time he put on his skates. Could he match his brilliance with the depth he knew was missing? Or would he fail tonight as he had always done? He felt the adrenalin surge into his body, his need to attain the impossible the dominant force in his mind.

Suddenly, the music exploded in the silence. The blue lights shattered the darkness, catching his body clad in scarlet pants and a wide leather belt over a bare chest and across one shoulder as he lifted into his first triple jump. His arms extended in a move that he had created, Jason stretched for the apex of the leap, fiercely determined no flaw would mar the aerial. He attained the perfect positioning, but the long sought for feeling wasn't there. This would not be the night, any more than any other that had gone before.

The sport that had become his life so many years ago was nothing but an empty shell of the effort, care, and dedication he had given to it. Betrayal of his gift and his skill was an acid burn in his thoughts. His eyes bleak, his mind coolly calculating his next move, he kept on skating, kept playing to the audience that had come to see the champion perform. They had paid top dollar for seats at the show. He had paid the cost with strained muscles, pain, emptiness, and weariness that no amount of rest assuaged; and a barren personal life that he could no longer tolerate. He raced down the ice, fleeing the images of the past, feeling the first bite of fear nipping at his heels. What if this was all there was to life? For one glorious moment, he felt something stir beneath the control he had perfected so carefully. Anger, soul-freeing anger. He shot off the ice, slamming through the air, riding the crest of the first sting of emotion. Even before he hit the top of the leap, the feeling died.

The audience sat spellbound at the brilliance he unleashed. Their collective breath caught, held, and then caught again. Sweat poured off his body. The light flashed over his damp skin, the muscles gleaming like warm, molten gold. Women poised on the edges of their seats, mesmerized by his male power and grace. Men felt inadequate before his skill. The critics would write later that nothing could top his performance. His agent, called to meet with Jason after the show, stood on the sidelines, mentally listing the sponsors who would be screaming for a chance to pay Jason's high fees for acting as spokesperson for their products.

Jason felt tendrils of human greed wrapping around him. The audience. Frank, his agent. Lisa, his female counterpart in the ice show and lover of three years in private. Each took from him. Each gave back a reflection of himself, emotionless, empty, barren. He finally knew that he had lived too long with the world taking bits of him with every performance, while he searched for that elusive dream called technical and emotional skating perfection. His breathing grew labored, his power seeping away. Superb training and his own ability to physically reach beyond himself drove him toward the finale. He felt the audience reach like a giant, greedy monster for the last of his essence. He responded, flying into the air, going higher, spinning faster than was safe. He landed, holding his edge, hearing their vicarious ecstasy as so much static. The lights were cut. The end of his performance had come and still the sound went on, waves of noise, cries for an encore. More tired than he had ever been, he listened to the announcer give the crowd more of his blood. His encore was pure flash and fire without heart. The audience saw only the glitz, not the absence of substance.

Finally, the performance was over amid even more cries for more. Ignoring the noise and the congratulations of his fellow skaters, Jason skated through the curtain, stopping only to put protectors over his blades before returning to his dressing room. The silence was as deep and without substance as the praise had been. He stood in the center of the room, his lips twisted grimly, his shoulders hunched in defeat. A knock sounded. Only two people, Lisa or Frank, would dare bother him after a show. He straightened, his face smooth as always, his eyes clear, unrevealing. Only a fool let his blood show in a sea filled with hungry sharks.

"Come in," he called as he sat down to take off his skates.

Frank surged through the door. "I couldn't believe my eyes. When you told me you wanted to see me, I couldn't think why. I never expected this kind of surprise. Do you have any idea what your stock in this country will be like tomorrow after that show? I spotted at least four major news people in the audience. I'll be able to sell you everywhere. The sky's the limit.'' Frank dropped into a chair, his ever-ready pad and pen busy with plans as he talked.

Jason stripped the stage makeup from his face, barely listening. He had called Frank to arrange a short leave from the ice show. Thinking his problems of late were mere weariness and dissatisfaction, he had intended few weeks' vacation. Now, he wondered if the problem were not deeper than that. He rose, took off his pants and tossed them over another chair before heading for the shower. Frank followed, still planning.

A few minutes later Jason returned to the main room of the star suite to pick up his street clothes. His wallet slipped from his slacks as another knock sounded at his door. This time it was Lisa, smiling, pleased with herself and the performance she had just finished.

''You better watch it, Iceman, the audience loved my act.'' She swayed toward him, taking a kiss that was usually her due.

''I always said you were dynamite on the ice,'' he murmured, kissing her lightly without feeling the slightest need to take more. Instead, he studied his reactions as though outside himself. He could see nothing in himself or Lisa that indicated any caring on either side. She, in her way, was just as self-motivated and ruled as he. Frank was a top man at his job, but had the sensitivity of a rock. Even now, the agent neither knew nor cared that Lisa was there. Nor did Lisa acknowledge the agent. Disturbed, wondering why he was suddenly given to introspection, Jason released Lisa. He turned away to pick up his dropped wallet. As he did, the leather opened to the picture section and the worn newspaper cutout of a young female skater caught in a beautiful leap. Jason studied the photo, remembering the moment and the girl.

Diana Diamond. A young phenomenon in her teens. She had been slated to win the gold four years after his medal but, inexplicably, she had quit cold the year before the Games. He touched the picture, thinking of the face, the wealth of joy and expression that had filled her every gesture the last time he had seen her skate. Her skill had been astoundingly fine-honed at her age, but her ability to interpret the music had been her true gift in his eyes. She had touched him and her audience. He had felt her in every fiber of his being that day. After that, nothing had been the same in his own skating. Because in looking at Diana, he had known his own lack.

"What have you got there?" Lisa asked, vaguely curious.

Jason closed the wallet and stuffed it in his slacks. Even to himself, he couldn't explain why he carried Diana's picture. "Nothing."

Lisa didn't press him further, instead asking, "Are we still going out tonight?"

He glanced at her, reading a faint discomfort in her stance. "Is there any reason we shouldn't?"

"Well, you've made it clear these past weeks . . ."

She stopped, smiling at her own hesitancy. "You know what I mean."

"You picked a strange time to bring this up."

She shrugged, going to the mirror to study her reflection. The costumer had done a great job with her new outfit. "Neither of us ever meant anything deep, nor are we the type to get upset over the end we both knew would come. I've been asked to dinner by the new skater. I want to go." She turned, looking him straight in the eyes. "I won't, unless we're done."

Jason searched for something in himself: regret, anger, pique, anything to tell him that the relationship he had shared with this woman for three years had touched him. He found nothing. The fear that had sprung up on the ice doubled, digging claws into his gut, demanding an answer before it was too late.

The strange thing was he had known their time together was over. "I should have told you weeks ago."

"Perhaps. I think I needed to see the end myself." She touched his arm, surprising them both with the unnecessary display. "You could have sent me packing. Thanks for letting it be this way."

Frank looked up. "Hey, you two. Are you almost done? I need to talk to Jason and then you can be alone."

Lisa dropped her hand. "No. You stay. I go."

Jason watched her walk out, making his first

ever impulsive decision. ''Frank, I want you to get me out of this contract with the show. Tonight's my last professional performance as a hired seal.''

ONE

Diana Diamond parked her car in the small slot near the office door of the ice skating rink. The night closed in around her as she got out, her boots crunching softly in the snow. She glanced up at the night sky, for a moment enjoying the gentle bite of the winter breeze on her face, the smell of pine in the air, and the silence that only three o'clock in the morning in Denver could bring. Knowing she couldn't afford to linger any longer if she was to make full use of her allotted ninety minutes of practice, she hurried inside. The building was empty except for two security guards and a lone skater working on his routine under the watchful eyes of his coach.

Denver boasted a number of rinks where professional skaters and amateurs could rent ice time. But of all of the establishments, Nicky's was the most in demand. The facility was a no-expense or amenity spared place with the extra bonus of not being open to the general public. The ice was always in better than good condition and the building quiet.

Diana sat down to slip on her skates, barely aware of the music coming from the tape machine on the table just outside the rink. The choreography she was designing for one of the top female professional skaters in the country held all of her attention. Despite the fact that she, in her own way, was as well-known as her clients, Diana still treated each routine she created as though it were the most important one she had ever tackled.

She looked up as the music ended, watching as the coach chastised his pupil about the quality of the final blur spin. The strident tone of voice the man used sent memories slashing through Diana's mind. How many times had she seen just such a situation? How many times had she been a recipient of this kind of lecture?

Once, she had had aspirations to chase the Olympic gold. Once, she had loved skating and performing. Audiences then had been fellow lovers of her sport and fans. She had wanted to do her best to bring alive the joy she had known on the ice. Later, that need to touch the hem of perfection had turned into a drive to win a medal in the Olympics. A series of coaches had entered her life. The first few had been wonderfully supportive, but each had been a bit tougher than the last, a bit more demanding and more critical. For a while, she had thrived on the challenge of bettering herself every time she skated. And then one day, one man had taught her perfection was a myth.

Shivering slightly, Diana shook her head, forcing the dark days back into the corners of her mind. She was no longer willing to relive those traumatic months in her life just before she had retired from competitive skating. That time was too painful, even now after ten years of civilian life. She had a career that she loved and she had tasted the reality of normal living. She was content, prosperous with a steadily growing clientele, and a healthy bank balance to match.

The sound of the man's harsh voice snagged her attention. She studied the pair in the center of the rink, her green eyes narrowed. Growing angry at the continued criticism, Diana bit back the words of rebuttal to which she had no right. A second later she got a surprise as the boy straightened beneath the barrage and answered back. She wanted to applaud him for having the courage she hadn't possessed at his age. The sudden silence was short before the coach grinned widely, clapped his protégé on the back in a kind of man-to-man agreement while saying something that Diana couldn't hear, but which brought a smile to the boy's face as they left together. Diana relaxed, glad to know this skater had a sympathetic coach, one who was honestly trying to help and not tearing a youngster's confidence to shreds for some reasons of his own.

Diana waited until she was alone before moving to the tape machine to put on her music. It was time she got down to business. She had spent the better part of a week listening to the piece she had chosen and outlining on paper the various moves she thought would work. Melinda, the woman for whom she was creating the routine, was a leggy, sultry soloist with dark eyes and the kind of body made for teasing a man. The fact that her personality lived up to the promise of her beauty made Diana's task much easier than it would have been had Melinda wanted to project a different image from her natural one on the ice.

Gliding to the center of the rink, Diana took her opening position and waited for the first note. Melinda was not very athletic, so the dance relied more on emotion than leaps and intricate maneuvers. The classical piece built gradually as Diana began with a slow glide a third of the way down from center. She thought herself into Melinda's skin, using every gesture she knew came naturally to the professional. Her head lifted, her black hair flirting with the lights that shone over her. She scanned the invisible crowd, finding that one man to whom to skate. Her body preened as the music built, the base in the melody growing stronger. Gauging her speed, she rose in a beautifully executed double toe loop, landing lightly as she slipped into a pattern of footwork that would show off Melinda's body in an undoubtedly skimpy costume to perfection. Her own unitard was pale green and figure hugging so that the effect was far more startling than anything Melinda would ever accomplish.

The music picked up, the spins and flashy turns grew in intensity. In the pool of light reflected off the ice, Diana seemed to come alive, blazing across the mirrored surface like living fire. Her head tossed, her eyes glittered with challenge, defiance, and the catch-me-if-you-can kind of dare designed to drive men wild. Her every move was a blatant invitation to delight and a picture of the abandon that burned in her soul.

Jason entered the rink, wondering what he was doing there. He had been traveling for most of the day. He was bone tired, hungry, and just plain exhausted—too exhausted to sleep. So he had come here instead of going to the apartment he had rented until he had time to look around for a more permanent setup. He nodded to the security guard he had met on his first trip to Nicky's before entering the huge room that housed the rink.

A wealth of sound poured over him. Music— rich, throbbing, demanding, and compelling—drew him down the aisle toward the spill of light glowing over the ice. A skater, clad in pale green, caught his eye. He stopped as she rose into the air in a twisting turn so beautiful he held his breath in admiration. She seemed to hang suspended for a heart-stopping moment before settling to earth again. Then, her smile flashed a wicked invitation that stirred more than his professional interest. Suddenly, his tired body found a new lease on life. The emotion this woman projected with her skating was unmistakable.

Diana Diamond. His nemesis. His obsession. Two long years of work, planning, and maneuvering to get to Denver, to find Diana, his dream and maybe, if he were lucky, a part of himself he needed to survive. But he had to be sure. So much rode on his strategy and Diana's involvement. Maybe he had idealized her talent and his own emptiness. Maybe she was just another skater.

His eyes narrowed to slits as he tried to find one flaw in her routine, something that would save him, give him an excuse to forget the plans that he had already put into motion. There was no flaw. Diana was pure passion on ice, emotion flowing from her to marry with the music that wrapped around her graceful body. Without even being aware of moving, he reached the edge of the rink, his hands settling on the wall separating them to bite into the polished wood.

His blood throbbed with the beat and every high-mettled toss of her head. Desire, never the ruler of his body, flashed through him, destroying years of discipline in one instant. His head lifted, his nostrils flaring as though he would catch her scent on the wind as a wild animal in search of a mate would have. No woman fragrance wrapped around him to welcome him into her dance. No inviting glance teased him nearer. The ice should have melted beneath the slashing blades of her skates, and yet it held. Rigid against the need he didn't want, the desire that hadn't been part of his plan, Jason watched Diana lift into a glorious jump, her body once again hanging there as though defying the very laws of nature before settling back to earth with such power and yet curious delicacy that he knew he had never seen better. The music swelled to a finish and Diana turned into a blur spin so perfectly executed he could see nothing but a flash of color twirling like an exquisite top.

The sound of his applause in the silence that followed startled them both. Diana came erect, her eyes wide with fear, and he mentally cursed the unplanned action for having betrayed his presence.

"Who's there?" Diana demanded breathlessly. With the lights on in the rink and the edges in darkness, she couldn't see. The security men for the building seldom watched her work as they had long since become bored with skaters in general. And visitors, unless authorized, were not permitted in the building.

Jason stepped into the light, his course set. There would be no going back. This woman held the key to the emotions he needed if he were ever to step back on the ice again. She could teach him what he had to learn. And if his plan was sound, she would never know that he had moved heaven, earth, and Frank to bring himself within her orbit to drink of her power. His plans for a comprehensive sports complex dedicated to figure skating was a long-held goal and now a camouflage for his private search.

Diana recognized him immediately. Despite the fact that Jason had retired from performing almost two years before, those rugged features had been depicted too often in both the sports and news magazines not to be known by almost anyone who kept up with athletic figures. Those eyes were as cold and expressionless in person as they appeared in print. The body was strong, straight, tall for a skater; but having seen him perform, Diana knew the grace and beauty of his work. His line was elegant, flawless.

Jason "Iceman" Starke. Brilliant technician. Superb athlete. Perfection on the silver blades. Olympic champion. World Champion three times. An American legend that every young male skater wanted to emulate, although few would ever attain his level of execution. He was all of that and probably more, and yet she couldn't rave about his work because it was so soulless, so empty of emotion. He gave nothing to the ice but perfection.

"Mr. Starke," Diana murmured finally, when it was clear he would not speak first.

Jason watched her study him. He saw the changing play of expressions. In her face, he could read every feeling that had never touched him. Diana was all that he had hoped and more. "You skate well," he said.

Her sudden reserve caught his attention. He had known, in fact anyone in the skating world knew, that Diana shunned the public eye, performances of any kind, and in general stayed out of the limelight at all costs. Her behavior had raised a great deal of speculation over the years as she had steadily climbed to the top of her profession. No one had ever found the answer to either her sudden retirement from amateur competition or her near fanatical determination to have nothing to do with amateur sports or performing again. Among other things, he meant to solve the mystery.

"Thank you," she replied absently, caught up in trying to figure out the man. No one could be this controlled. Yet, as Jason moved toward her, she found nothing in his eyes to change her image of him. He could have been a breathing statue for all the change in his expression. That mouth, though beautifully formed, was straight, without a hint of a curve to indicate that he had ever smiled. His voice was deep and mellow, but so even and free of expression it could have come from a very sophisticated machine. Diana wrapped her arms around herself as he stopped less than a foot away. Suddenly, she felt cold.

"You shouldn't stand around in these temperatures after that kind of exertion. You'll stiffen up." He shrugged out of his topcoat and offered it to her.

Diana shook her head. "I have a jacket over there."

He glanced in the direction in which she pointed and shifted his shoulders. "It's doing a good job of keeping the bench warm." He took the final step that would bring him within touching distance and draped the coat over her shoulders. Her skating had been breathtaking, but she was even more so. The combination of green eyes, ebony hair, and matte white skin was as near to perfection as he had seen. Her scent surrounded him, teasing his senses as desire slammed into his midsection. The faint spicy fragrance of her cologne was delicate, clean, and clearly meant more for the pleasure of wearing than seduction. And yet, he was coming alive despite his best efforts at control. Irritation warred with a very real desire to touch her. Stifling both, he concentrated on words. In his determination to stay the captain of his own being, he neglected his verbal messages. The first words from his mouth betrayed all that he would hide.

"Are you married or otherwise engaged?"

Diana jerked back, stunned at the blunt question. She had read Jason Starke would wander where even the devil would not go, but she hadn't expected this. "Why?" she demanded.

Although he had blundered badly, Jason used his mistake to advantage. "Why do you think? You appeal to me. I don't poach. Better to know if there is someone before I ask." Her surprise was genuine he decided. Odd. He would have thought she would be accustomed to male attention.

Diana knew if she hadn't gained at least the appearance of poise in her twenty-nine years of existence that her jaw would have dropped at his almost indifferent delivery. "Look, Mr. Starke, I don't know where you have gotten the idea I would welcome your interest, but I don't. You may be a big man on the ice, but I don't know you from Adam's house cat."

"I thought that was what dating was all about, getting to know one another," he observed, more curious at her reluctance than her refusal.

"Dating?" Twin dark brows rose skeptically.

"I never asked you to bed," he pointed out.

Diana stared, wondering if three a.m. skating

had turned her brains to lumpy oatmeal. He couldn't have said that. ''I wouldn't have gone.''

''Of course not. You're a woman who likes knowing who she's with.'' He wrapped his fingers around her arm and urged her toward the bench where her coat and shoes lay. Her skin was warm, yielding and yet firm in his grasp. As with every other woman he had ever known, the effect should have been nothing more than pleasant interest. It was, instead, as though he had caught hold of something alive, compelling, and addictive. He wanted to slide his fingers beneath the fabric that shielded her from his touch. He wanted to stroke the long length of her arm, find the tiny nerves that created delight, and knead the muscles that had given her such grace and beauty on the ice. Dampening his need had never been so hard, but he succeeded. He kept his grip light and his mind focused on the conversation.

''What *are* you doing?''

''Hopefully, moving you from here to somewhere warm, preferably with facilities to make a decent cup of coffee. I've been traveling most of the day and I need something to keep me vertical.''

''I am not going anywhere.'' She pulled her arm from his grasp with more force than his light hold required. Prepared for resistance, she lost her balance. Jason caught her as her feet started to go out from under her and pulled her tight against him. Diana tipped back her head to stare into his eyes. They were analytical rather than admiring. Once again, she felt that coldness as almost a physical caress. She had never seen so unemotional a person in her life.

Jason looked for her reaction, hoping for an answering response in himself. Something stirred, faint but there. He both welcomed and fought the change. He had chosen a dangerous road, he decided, as he gazed into her eyes. Could he control the future as he had always done, as he had always needed to do? He hadn't come for the woman, only the professional.

"You're beautiful." Her eyes weren't plain green, rather the deep evergreen of the forest. Dark, mysterious, a perfect hiding place for the secrets of a woman.

"And you're a crazy man," she returned, fighting the warmth of his body stealing through her clothes and the firm feel of his arms around her. She had little or no use for people who could not or would not express their feelings. The fact that his words were touching her, drawing a response she hadn't expected, angered her.

Her body felt good against his, Jason decided. She was just the right size to hold as his own quickening in certain very definite regions attested to. "An interesting reaction to a compliment," he murmured, shifting so she would not be aware of how near to the edge he was. He needed her cooperation, not her wariness.

"I don't see a compliment. I hear a statement of fact in your opinion." She tried to push out of his arms, but got nowhere. Whatever else the man might be, he was strong with muscles made tight and hard by hours of practice. She would be free only if she made a scene or he decided to release her. Since she wasn't prepared for the first possibility, she would have to wait him out. The fact did little to help her slowly building temper. It had been a long time since anyone had had the nerve to try to bully her.

He studied her, feeling the change in her mood as though she had told him aloud. "You're angry. Why?"

"You would be, too, if you could hear what I hear. I am not a thing. Stop talking to and about me as if I were."

He frowned, surprised at the biting retaliation. "Was I doing that?"

At the honest puzzlement in his voice, the first hint of any emotion, Diana went still. She had thought his behavior a practiced, unfeeling technique for getting a woman. From his reaction, it appeared as if she were wrong. Wary, suspecting a trick but having a sinking feeling that Jason wasn't putting on an act, she asked, "What would you have called it?"

The question was reasonable, even logical, given the circumstances. But it was also something he didn't want to answer. Releasing her, he stepped back, mentally cursing his stupidity for having allowed himself to be sidetracked. "What you called it, obviously. I just didn't expect you to catch me out. Bad habit, I guess."

Diana almost believed him. The voice was

smooth, patently sincere, the eyes steady and clear. But something, a feel for people, the sensitivity that had been her curse from birth, told her Jason was lying. Always one for the underdog, the hurt or the unloved, she let her need to nurture and comfort overrule logic. Despite evidence to the contrary, she had a feeling that Jason was in need. She didn't know the source, but she could feel an emptiness that, somehow, she was sure he was trying to fill.

"I must finish practicing."

Jason saw a strange warmth replace the temper in her eyes, a warmth that no one but Lorelei and Pippa had ever offered him. Once, he had tried to love both women, one his sister and the other his aunt, but couldn't despite the fact that they loved him and made no secret of their feelings. There had been too many in his life who used him to further themselves, their dreams, or to bask in reflected glory. He had killed the ability to love, lost the need to trust. Where there had been emotion, vulnerability, there was now only logic and reason. He believed only in what he could see, touch or taste, and what he could do. He had earned his nickname honestly. He was encased in ice and he kept the freezer on high. He didn't want this woman to look at him with heat. He didn't need her to reach out to him except as he had planned. He didn't want commitments, entanglements, or relationships. He only wanted to achieve depth for his skating.

"I need to get some rest." He turned to walk away.

"My name's Diana."

Her soft voice stopped him. He glanced over his shoulder to find her still watching him. Another mistake. He had forgotten to ask her name. He should have because there was no way that he could logically explain that he had known who she was without betraying how closely he had traced her career. Diana Diamond's face was rarely seen in print these days.

"You never did ask, you know."

"I should have. I'm sorry." The first words were born of his original intent. The second emerged out of a tiny burst of emotion. Irritated, he bit back an oath. Apologies were for the weak and those they sought to impress.

"You also forgot your coat. It's cold out."

Now there was concern in her eyes. A faint anger displaced annoyance. He was a stranger. How could she care that he might need his coat? Had he read her wrong? Was she trying to impress him? "I've been colder."

Diana glided forward, torn between thinking herself crazy for prolonging the meeting and needing to touch this man in a way that would put a tiny crack in his control. "But not because of me." She lifted the coat from her shoulders to drape it over his. But even with the added height of her skates, she couldn't quite reach him. "You'll have to bend down." She watched his face, searching for the smallest hint of expression. His eyes were steady, dark, and still.

He shook his head, his hands coming up to take it from her.

"I don't bite." She couldn't give up.

He paused, startled at her soft declaration. "Why do you care?"

She almost smiled at the flicker of surprise. She had done it. "Why shouldn't I?"

Without realizing it, his stance softened slightly, his voice deepened. "I'm a stranger."

"You're a person."

He mentally drew back at that. "A bleeding-heart type."

The words stung as Diana suspected he meant them to. "I've been called worse." She didn't understand Jason, but she could comprehend that he was trying to push her away. "Bend down before we both freeze."

Jason studied her, seeing what he had missed earlier. There was spirit and courage in those green eyes. Diana was barely five-feet-three inches and she was used to getting her own way. Unless he was ready to wrestle her for the right to help him with his own coat, the woman was prepared to stand in front of him for the rest of the night or for as long as it took. His mouth twitched at the image. Pippa would love this one.

Diana caught her breath as the smile dawned on his lips. It was like watching the birth of a new day after the total darkness of a moonless night. Slowly, his gaze holding hers every step of the way, Jason bent his six-foot-four height down to her level. His face just inches from her own, Diana dropped the coat over his shoulders.

For one moment, he stared into her eyes, the urge to taste her lips so strong that he almost weakened. But it was the very strength of his response that gave him the push to pull back. To want because he was hungry was one thing, to want because he needed was impossible to accept. He lifted his head, his control firmly in place. "You are entirely too trusting. As you said, you don't know me."

Diana drew back, watching his cold eyes move over her. There was no way to miss the insult in his gaze, nor any way to stem her anger at his behavior.

"If I weren't a lady, I'd slap you for that," she whispered.

"Anyone who knows me would warn you I'm no gentleman." He had succeeded in killing her interest, but he felt his first twinge of doubt at his tactics.

Diana backed away, shaking her head. "One day I'll learn about leading with my heart," she muttered, disgusted with herself for being taken in.

Jason knew she hadn't meant for him to hear. His fingers clenched into a fist as she continued to put distance between them. With every increasing inch of space, her warmth receded, leaving him cold. Suddenly, she knew the meaning of loneliness, his second lesson at Diana's hands.

The light in the center of the rink gathered

around her, a beckoning sun as he stood in the darkness watching. She straightened, her gaze holding his for one instant. The regret and pain he could see in her eyes slipped beneath his guard, cracking the coldness in his heart. Before he could act, she turned to the tape machine and restarted the music. The sound poured into the silence as she moved into the beat. He knew he should leave and knew he would stay to see her dance.

Diana threw herself into the music, feeling battered in a way she couldn't have explained if asked. A stranger. Hurting, she suspected, although she couldn't have said how. She was so lost in thought that she forgot she was skating as Melinda and let her own personality shine through. Few saw her as herself these days. The claws of the past were still buried deep in her being. Angry, confused, her blades sliced over the ice. She attacked the leaps, flinging her body into the air, defying the man who watched her, challenging him through the skill they both understood. The music was her silver thread to mother earth, her passion was her wings to the freedom of flight. Her eyes glittered with the fire of her emotions as she soared, twisted, and turned over the frozen surface. Every move she made was played to him and that angered her, too. She shouldn't have cared.

Jason's eyes followed her over the ice. Without realizing it, his breath quickened. He could feel her straining for the impossible, challenging him in every chance she took. He had never seen a female skater with such power. Her skill was without equal, but her power was as untamed as a volcano in full eruption. And yet, there was grace, too, in spite of the anger and hurt that drove her. The routine was much more intricate than the first one. The leaps higher, more risky, the arm extensions complete and so beautiful he could have been watching a prima ballerina. Her passion was no woman's wiles set to music, but femininity personified within the confines of the icy stage. He searched again for a flaw in her technique and found none. His admiration tripled as the music swelled to a finish and she lifted into the most difficult of the jumps she had done so far. For a skater to have this kind of strength and power at the end of a routine indicated superb conditioning. But, as she hung over the unforgiving surface of the ice, he felt a bite of fear he had never known. Without realizing it, he stepped forward as she hurtled toward the landing. She couldn't hold the edge. No one could. But Diana did, her arms outstretched as though she would embrace the world.

Mesmerized, stunned at the way his heart had quickened in fear for her, Jason froze, his eyes holding hers. The music went silent and once again they were facing each other.

"Why don't you perform in public?" he demanded, asking one of the questions he had been unable to answer in all his research. His voice was no longer smooth, expressionless. Neither of them noticed.

Diana was breathing heavily as she stood in the

center of the rink. She cursed the fact that because
he had been there her skating had been fired with
more power than she had ever felt. It had been a
long time since she had been able to skate before
an audience, no matter how small, without the fear
that had become her constant companion ten years
ago. Tonight, her anger and hurt had made the
past a forgotten memory. She had stepped into the
circle of light, trapped in her emotions, and finding once more, for fleeting moments, the sheer
magnificence of the empty ice, the cascade of
sound and the freedom of skating.

"Because I don't choose to," she answered
flatly.

TWO

Jason wasn't spoiled by his success, but he had lived in a world where those who inhabited it with him had treated him with respect and deference. This woman showed him neither. Annoyed with her attitude, his eyes narrowed as he took a step toward her.

"Are you always so rude when someone asks a question?" he said sarcastically.

"You didn't ask. You commanded an answer." She faced him, seeing emotion now that had not been present before. Her senses sprang to life at the knowledge that she had made a dent in his unbelievable control.

He digested that, testing it for truth or a woman's evasion. "All right. I'll rephrase the question. Why would a woman with your obvious skill and talent refuse to share it with others by performing?"

"Not everyone likes the limelight," she replied evasively.

Jason watched her, wondering how far to push.

So much rode on getting her attention and convincing her to help him with the complex. "You did once," he murmured carefully.

Diana blinked at the soft tone that could have been a prelude to a seduction—hers. If he hadn't been looking straight at her, had he been a stranger to her in reputation, she might have been taken in by the husky voice. But his eyes gave him away. They were shrewd rather than admiring, testing rather than alive with male curiosity. She should have been angry at the way he was playing with her. She should have walked away and left him to the games she didn't understand and wouldn't have participated in had she known the rules. Instead, she found she couldn't turn her back on him. Something held her still, perhaps a wild creature caught by the glare of a hunter's artificial light.

"What are you doing here?" she asked finally, feeling that there was something she should know, but having no idea what. Uneasy, wary, she tried to tell herself that it was the night, the silence, and the man that were causing the effect.

"I'm visiting with an eye to relocation." A partial truth was enough for now. He was a step closer and carefully eliminating the distance between them.

"Why?" She raised her head to maintain eye contact as he stopped once again before her. This time, there was no coldness in him to protect her from the impact of the man.

At another time, he would have had the clarity of mind to take advantage of this informal setting to begin his campaign. But facing Diana, feeling the first sting of emotions long dead now resurrected, had scrambled his thoughts and wrecked havoc with his control. Too much rode on his plans. "A long story and we don't have time now, and I'm too tired to make much sense."

Diana tipped her head, judging the truth from the evasion she only sensed. She was beginning to read him and that bothered her. "You know who I am," she murmured at last, saying the only thing that made sense. She knew she was gaining a reputation but that Jason, from his exalted position, should know of her was a shock.

A masterpiece of understatement, he thought. Diana Diamond was a sought-after gem for almost every skater in the country, and possibly quite a few in the world. Many of the would-be greats waited in the wings for just a chance at one of her routines, while stars paid exorbitant sums for her time and creativity.

"Was it a secret? Despite the fact that you stay out of the public eye as much as possible, you aren't invisible nor without reputation," he said, letting his very real admiration for her talent show. He wanted to soothe her wariness. He wanted her answers not her questions. "Although I'm not certain 'ice wizardess' suits you."

Diana relaxed slightly as the strange feeling of being stalked receded. "If others see me as some sort of ice wizardess," she grimaced as she used the nickname that the newspapers had given her when so many of her clients had begun to take awards and medals with her routines, "then that's their problem. Not mine."

He inclined his head. "Fame isn't all it's reputed to be. There always seems to be thorns in the roses we're thrown," he murmured.

Diana missed the watchful gleam in his eyes as she responded. "You don't have a reputation for acting as if it matters to you."

"Weakness is like blood in shark-infested waters. One sign of either and there are people just waiting to have your heart on a platter," he stated flatly, the words coming from the core of his being, uncensored by the restraint of mind and feeling that he usually exercised.

Diana sighed deeply, soundlessly. He was human after all. For a moment, she had been convinced Jason was indeed the Iceman he had been dubbed. Instead, he was a man who had been taught the hard way the price of success. She could understand that, having been burned herself.

"Are you finished with practice now?"

"Yes."

"The offer for coffee is still open." He tossed the invitation out casually, not wanting to spook her again.

Diana tipped her head, studying him, aware of the subtle shifting of moods. "You were angry before . . ."

"Masculine pique. I like to think myself unaffected by the groupies and the hangers-on, but I guess I'm not." He shrugged, vaguely surprised to discover he felt badly about what he was intending. If he hadn't known of Diana's aversion to anything to do with amateur skating, he would have preferred an honest approach to his offer for her to join the team he was putting together for the sports complex.

"Logic tells me I shouldn't believe you."

"You don't strike me as a logical woman," he returned as though giving the matter some thought. Tiredness was seeping deeper into his body, making his brain work twice as hard for the right words. Regret strengthened, spawning doubt that he rarely felt.

She smiled at that. "I'm not."

He watched her lips, finding, once again, hunger that had nothing to do with his reasons for seeking out Diana. God, she was so wary and yet so open to hurt. Although he was no longer prey to either sensation, he remembered the bite of both. He didn't want to hurt her even to help himself. Driven by an impulse to warn her, he spoke harshly, "On second thought, I think you'd be safer being logical. And I'd be better off getting some rest." He forced his feet to move away from her smile and the need to stay near. He was capable of a lot of things, but lying to this woman wasn't on the list. His research had armed him with most of the particulars about her past and her reaction to the events that had shaped her. He knew what he wanted of her would be hard for her even to consider, and what he needed of her almost impossible to explain.

Diana watched him head for the door, puzzled

at the abrupt withdrawal. "Jason, wait," she called, pausing only long enough to slip on blade protectors over her skates.

"Leave it, Diana," Jason replied without stopping. If he didn't go now, he might forget his plans, her past, and what she would think of him if she knew what he intended to do. "Forget I came here."

"Why?" she demanded, putting her hand on his arm so he would have to face her or shake her off.

He halted then, angry that she wouldn't let him, for once in his life, put someone else's needs before his own. He whirled around, not even noticing her hand dropping from his shoulder. If he hadn't been so tired, he might have kept his temper. "You didn't ask how I came to be here at this hour. You should have."

Diana frowned at the vehemence in his voice. There was nothing controlled about Jason now. He looked ready to splatter the rink with emotion. Fire, anger, regret, and frustration were almost palpable forces around them. "I must be dense, but I don't know what you're talking about."

"A skating school. For Olympians. Here. At Nicky's." The words snapped off his tongue like miniature whips. Diana flinched from each one. "Specifically, a figure-skating complex complete with dorms, coaches, choreographers, trainers, sports psychologists, and costumers. You're at the top of my list for recruitment."

Diana stared at him with horror-filled eyes, every one of the dark memories of the past coming back in vivid color to haunt her. "You can't mean that. Nicky would have told me." She stared at him, reading the truth in his eyes. "I won't help you," she whispered, feeling trapped and betrayed.

He nodded, showing no surprise at her response. "There are still scars. I was warned you wouldn't have any part of my plans, even though you're the best for the job. You've been there. You know what these children go through sometimes as they try to reach for the impossible. You stood in front of a bunch of newspaper people and spoke of a one-dimensional life, the demands of training, the need to find something beyond the confines of the rink. You've made it clear since that you don't want anything to do with amateur sports. One could say you are almost rabid on the subject."

Diana backed away from the words as much as from the man.

Jason followed her retreat. "You gave up a chance for the gold just to escape. You avoid anything that has to do with the beginning levels of our profession. Your attitude is as famous as your expertise. With your seal of approval on my training complex, I would automatically lift public opinion higher than years of practice in the field. I'm a newcomer, a man perhaps with dreams too impractical for reality. With your help and others like you, I could be taken seriously. I want to do more than just teach kids how to skate and win competitions. I want to give them a place to grow as individuals and skaters."

His confession, despite its delivery, caught her

attention as nothing else could have. On the one hand, she was angry at the information he had deliberately withheld from her; and yet, on the other, she found she couldn't deny being impressed by his intention to walk away, even when she had been on the verge of accepting his invitation without being aware of his motives. "Did you expect to find me here tonight?"

"How could I? I didn't know what practice time you used."

"You could have asked Nicky."

"I could have," he agreed wearily, rubbing the back of his neck as he watched her.

Diana felt her sympathy stir at the gesture. "You look done in."

"I hate traveling," he stated bluntly, his voice rough with fatigue. There it was again, that soft heart aimed in his direction. Her gentleness was beguiling, making him want to yield when he needed to stay tough. He resented it even as he basked in the warmth.

"Then why did you come here instead of getting some rest?"

"I also hate strange beds and I was too tired to sleep." His dark eyes pinned her, mocking her sympathy and her questions. "Going to offer to mother me?"

She shook her head. Jason was like a bramble patch. He was loaded with thorns without one flower to temper the image. "Not in your dreams. You don't need a mother. You need someone with an iron heart."

His brows rose at the description. "You can tell that by just a few minutes of talking to me?"

"I'm not the only one with a reputation," she reminded him.

He grimaced, knowing just how bad his character reading often was in the press. Despite having been retired from professional skating for almost two years, his name still appeared more often than he liked. "You can't always believe everything you see in print."

"I don't. But I also know that usually there is at least some truth to those kind of stories."

"Which ones? The women or the competitiveness?"

"Both, I suppose. But that isn't what bothers me. I've watched you skate and I saw so much potential for true greatness, if the moves hadn't been done by a human robot. Don't you ever let yourself feel anything on the ice? I could understand that kind of thing in the amateur competitions, but not when you turned pro and had greater artistic freedom."

He drew back, not expecting the lash of criticism. "You didn't read those papers all that well, if you don't remember that was supposed to be my greatest flaw. Brilliant technician, I believe, is the term usually applied. 'His skating is diamond hard and just as sharp' was one of my favorite quotes," he flared angrily. He should have allowed for her perception, her sensitivity.

"You could have changed that. You had the

ability," she returned sharply. The artist in her was too curious to let the subject alone.

"And you could have gone on with your skating if you hadn't chickened out at the last minute. Twelve years of training! You were on the verge of being on the Olympic team, slated to place in the top three that year, if not bring home the gold and you bailed out. Don't talk to me about freedom. At least I lived up to my commitments, and didn't let down those who believed in me and worked for and with me." Until that moment, he hadn't realized how betrayed he had felt when she had bailed out.

Diana hurt so much from his summation that she hit back without thinking. The self truth she had discovered later, at great cost, rather than at the time, erupted in a spate of words. "I walked out to avoid becoming what you are. I wanted to remember how to cry and to laugh and to get angry. I didn't want to live to skate, and I sure didn't want to forget how to be human enough to get tired. We may be skaters, but we aren't machines." She whirled around, more angry and hurt than she had ever been in her life. Nicky should have told her the place was up for sale, if for no other reason than she would have to find another rink to use. With one stroke, Jason Starke had ripped her life wide open.

"Don't you ever face anything, lady?" Jason called after her.

"Plenty. More than you probably, Mr. Iceman. And don't ever call me lady again," she shouted back as she plopped down on the bench to remove her skates with jerky, temper-driven motions. The sound of the door slamming was both pleasing and curiously deflating. She shouldn't have gotten angry. Equally, she shouldn't have allowed herself to be taken in by Jason's polished act. Once again, her defender-of-the-underdog personality had held sway over logic and commonsense.

"But no more," she promised herself aloud. "You did me a good turn, Iceman, by letting me in on your little game. I won't be such easy pickings next time." She gathered her things and slipped into her long coat. She left the rink through the side door, stopping short on finding Jason leaning against her car.

"What do you want?" she demanded irritably, wondering what trick he would use now.

"Hopefully, a ride. I came in a taxi." He nodded toward the single suitcase sitting at his feet in the snow. "It's late, and as you pointed out, I've had it. Waiting for a cab at this hour doesn't appeal. I'd probably fall flat on my face asleep in the snow and freeze to death."

"Some of us wouldn't think that was all that great a loss," she muttered.

His nod and slight smile caught her off guard. She stared at him, watching, waiting for the catch she knew was in here somewhere.

"I deserved that," he said ruefully. He spread his hands, watching her as carefully as she did him. He hadn't known he was capable of more than a momentary regret for anything. In the space

of a few minutes, he had run the gauntlet of more
emotion than he had felt in the last ten years. He
still didn't understand what it was about this woman
that made him feel so much, but he couldn't afford
to let her out of his sight until he solved the riddle.
"On the other side of the coin, I figure you owe
me one. My little knight-errant act in letting you in
on my strategy wasn't the smartest move for me."

"That's your problem."

If he couldn't get to her one way, he'd try
another. "I didn't think you were afraid of me."

"I'm not," she denied instantly. "And don't try
that bit about proving it."

He grinned, suddenly liking her smart retorts
and unbending stand. Diana Diamond had courage
and nerve. "If I promise to behave? I won't mention the skating complex. In fact, I won't even talk
if you like."

"I don't trust you."

There was a faint softening in her voice. The
elation that should have come with knowing he
had won was missing. All he felt was a strange
sense of relief. "Good. You shouldn't. Given half
a chance, I might take advantage. I've been doing
it so long that it's second nature to me these
days."

"Don't be nice. I don't trust that either."

He shrugged, feeling as though he had come a
long way in a short time. "Don't worry. It doesn't
last long."

Diana didn't want to laugh. But not wanting to
do something and actually succeeding were two

different things, she realized as a grin started to form. She looked at the lean frame draped over her little compact and knew she was going to let him ride with her. She was a soft-hearted fool, but he looked ready to drop from exhaustion despite his tough words.

"I don't think you can hold out for that long," she murmured resignedly.

Jason pushed himself erect, determined this time to stick to the terms of their bargain. "I don't think I could under ordinary conditions, but tonight I know I'll keep my word." He waited while she unlocked his side of the car first.

Diana steeled herself against the appeal in his fatigue-roughened voice. She would not allow herself to be taken in again. Jason Starke was a lethal combination in any form, but the most appealing side of him was pure poison for her. That weary expression called on every feminine instinct within her to provide succor. She wanted to touch him, to soothe that muscled body, and erase those deep lines of exhaustion from his face.

"Don't just stand there, get in," she commanded irritably. "And don't fall asleep before you tell me where you're staying or so help me, I'll tip you out in the snow."

Jason grinned tiredly at the nonsense tripping off her tongue. This woman wouldn't turn away anyone who needed her, although she would probably make a good attempt at scratching his eyes out if he had the nerve to say as much. "I rented a place in that new condo complex in the foothills. Do you know it?''

''Yes.'' Diana inserted the key in the ignition, wondering how one perfectly adequate car could suddenly become so cramped. Her arm was almost intimately entwined with Jason's. She could hear every tiny shift he made to get comfortable and the interior was already warming up from their shared body heat. His scent was rich, a combination of expensive cologne and pure male. And she was in big trouble, trouble spelled T-R-O-U-B-L-E.

Diana guided the car onto the street, waiting for Jason to reopen the conversation on the complex. She didn't put any stock at all in his promise to remain silent. When four miles went by and he still hadn't spoken, she began to reevaluate. Risking a sidelong glance at his relaxed form, she found his eyes closed, his breathing so even that she began to suspect he had fallen asleep on her. Annoyed when she should have been relieved that he wasn't pressing the sports-complex issue, she returned her attention to the road.

Jason watched Diana from the screen of his lashes. Her expressions, what little he could see of them from the intermittent illumination from the street lights, was a mixture of emotions. The predominant one was relief. It didn't take more than one guess to know she had been braced to fend off any attempt he made to discuss the complex. He frowned inwardly at the mess he had made tonight. His exhaustion and the impulse to check out Nicky's had a lot to answer for. He had to retrieve his position, but at the moment he didn't have a clue as to how. As for his curiosity about Diana, that, too, seemed destined to be fraught with obstacles.

Diana Diamond had clearly built herself a life based on her past and her own ideas of what the future would hold. She could be touched emotionally, but from what he had learned of her professional dealings and what he had seen tonight, once she made up her mind, there was no arguing with her. As much as that characteristic was a problem now, if he could bring her into his plans, that trait would then become one of his greatest assets. Diana had a strength of will he could admire.

Diana pulled to a stop in front of a luxury condo complex, vaguely noting the natural wood and glass construction that was so popular in the area. She turned slightly in the seat to study Jason. True to his word, he hadn't said anything during the trip. As far as she could tell, he was asleep. She waited a moment, hoping the change of motion would awaken him. When he continued to slumber, apparently unaware, she bit her lip trying to decide what to do. The easiest thing should have been to shake him awake, but she just couldn't make herself do it. He looked so peaceful now that the lines of weariness were smoothing from his face. The hard glint of purpose in his eyes was hidden behind dark, blunt lashes. His hands were still, his long body relaxed as though it had never been pushed to the limits of its capabilities.

Her gaze slipped over him, hunting for an answer to the way she felt drawn to him. Even now, knowing his plans for the rink, she couldn't make herself pull away. He was cold, emotionally, mentally. He was hard, sharp, and clearly a man more interested in results than the way they were obtained. In short, he combined all the things she didn't like in one package. Annoyed with her own inconsistency, she placed her hand on his shoulder and shook him once.

"Come on, Starke, we're here."

Jason made a pretense of waking up. He had kept his promise, but it had been hard. The ride had given him a chance to think, but not an opportunity to come up with a solution to the situation in which he found himself. So, he had played dead, figuratively. He had known the moment she had decided he was really asleep and had relaxed. And just now he had felt her puzzlement over something that had to do with him.

"Jason, get up. It's late and I want to get home." In her need to get him out of her car, Diana leaned closer so her eyes were level with his. When his opened, she found herself impaled by the dark light she could barely see. "It's time to get out," she whispered.

Jason studied her, hoping she wouldn't move away and wishing she hadn't come so close. "I know. Come out with me tomorrow. Dinner?"

"No."

"Why not? I'm no danger to you now that you know why I'm here." He lifted his hand slowly, watching her carefully. She didn't move away, but she did flinch when he cupped her cheek lightly in his palm.

"I meant what I said. I don't trust you."

"And I meant what I said. Don't. But there is one thing you can trust. Dinner tomorrow, or tonight actually, and I'll behave. No tricks. My word. A truce, if you like."

She searched his eyes, seeing truth where there had been no emotion a second before. "I didn't know we were at war."

He smiled slowly.

She inhaled sharply at the sight. Every objection she had flew right out of her head at the change in his face. He looked younger, less tough, intensely masculine, but with a gentleness that added to that male image rather than sat curiously detached from it.

"We are. We both want different things and neither of us usually loses. I have a feeling there is a confrontation in our future, Diana Diamond, but it won't come over dinner tonight."

"But what will come over dinner?" she asked, knowing she was going to agree whether it was the smart thing to do or not.

"Understanding. Maybe liking. Maybe more. I don't know. Does it matter that much to you to have all the answers before the questions are asked?"

"It has before."

"And I've never led with my emotional chin before. Your risk against mine."

Their eyes met and held, both searching for a way through the maze of uncertainties.

"All right."

"Seven."

"You don't know where I live."

His smile died. For one moment, he stared at her as he came to a decision. Stealth and tricks would not win her. Oh, he might get her name on a contract, but he wouldn't get the passions that burned in her with incandescent heat. And the second was more important than the first. He turned, reaching for the case lying on the seat behind him. Unlocking it, he lifted the lid an inch, and extracted a thin folder before resecuring the lock. He dropped the folder into Diana's lap.

"I know where you live, your phone number, and the license of this car, among other things."

Diana stared first at him then at the papers. "What's this?" she asked, having a terrible feeling she knew.

"Research." He didn't flinch from her accusing look.

She glanced down, knowing she was going to open the folder and hating the fact that she was aware of its existence. "You had no right."

"We both know differently. We give up the right to privacy when we become public figures. You may choose to keep your face out of the camera's eye, but that doesn't mean you aren't a public figure."

The light in the car was slight, but not so faint

that Diana couldn't read the facts of her life reduced to lines of words on a page.

"The only thing I couldn't get hold of was a recent picture, and believe me, I tried."

She raised her eyes to his, trying without success to understand him. "Why are you telling me this now?"

His lips twisted at the question. "I don't like manipulating you. So, I'm giving you a head start, I guess. I want you for the complex and I won't give up. But I will play fair, hard but fair."

"A warning?"

"A promise. I always keep those." He smiled faintly. "Even I have a few rules I live by. Are you willing to risk getting close to me or will you fight me by running?"

"I don't think giving you my back would be a smart move."

His smile became a grin of pure enjoyment. "Smart lady."

She laughed, discovering that the folder wasn't all that terrible after all. "If you're late, I won't wait," she returned, doing some warning of her own.

He chuckled softly. "I didn't think you would."

THREE

Diana stared out the window of her home, watching the light powder of snow dust the landscape. It was almost noon, a strange hour for a person to start a day, but that was the way her life was set up. She skated from three a.m. to four-thirty, came home to sleep until ten, took a short walk to wake up properly, then she did what little housework and chores were required to keep the two bedroom, one bath house she had purchased two years ago running smoothly. Lunch was at two, then she worked on her routines, selecting music for new numbers, planning on paper the moves needed to marry skater and music together in one unbreakable bond of beauty and skill. Dinner was between seven and eight, a short nap, and then she was ready for the rink. Depending on the season, she fit in a ski run, horseback trail ride, or nature walk into each day, a gift to herself for the disciplined life she led. Otherwise, her hours were given to her work and her home. She didn't own a pet, in fact, had never thought about getting one. Her friends tended to be in the profession and, therefore, accustomed to the discipline that was so much a part of her. She sometimes regretted her relatively narrow lifestyle but, with the exception of the year she had set the skating world on its ear by bailing out, as Jason put it, she found a curious kind of contentment in the structure.

But lately, she also found boredom and such a feeling of repetition that she had been toying with cutting down on the number of clients she handled or taking on an apprentice. Neither course particularly appealed for various reasons. She massaged her temples lightly as she watched the snow and considered the situation that now existed because of Jason Starke. Whether she wanted it or not, she would have to make a change. To avoid being exposed to the man and his plans, she would need another place to skate. But first, she had to talk to Nicky. More to the point, she was in the mood to give him a taste of her temper for not having warned her of the change on the horizon. Rising, she went to the closet for her coat. Nicky would be at the rink by now.

"Is he in?"

"Diana, what are you doing here this early?" Maggie, Nicky's secretary and wife, asked.

"Doing my best to hold onto my temper. Your boss has been playing fast and loose with me."

Maggie's jaw dropped momentarily before she recovered. "Nicky? Our Nicky? Impossible."

"Yes, our Nicky."

"Do I hear my name being taken in vain?" Nick Minolti, better known as Nicky, wandered out of his own office into his wife's. He was a short little gnome of a man with smiling eyes, a quick temper, and a love of ice skating and those who sacrificed for the sport.

Diana swung around, sternly eyeing the man she had called friend for years. "Why didn't you tell me about Jason Starke and the sale?" she demanded.

Nicky blinked owlishly, his hazel eyes looking even more vague than usual. "I thought I had."

"Don't give me that forgetful expression. You *know* you didn't."

Nicky shifted uncomfortably under her narrow-eyed stare. He glanced at his wife and almost cringed at her hot-tempered look. "He made it a condition of the sale," he said speaking to both women and then adding to his wife, "You know we wanted to sell." He turned to Diana. "And if he hadn't been so adamant about making sure that your skate time was guaranteed, even that wouldn't have been enough. He's even locking in your rates, Diana, for as long as he owns the rink." He pulled out the condition hoping to mitigate the anger he could see building in her eyes. And he hoped it would temper his wife's ire that she hadn't been told.

"I can't believe all this is going on under my nose and you didn't tell me," Maggie protested vigorously, glaring at her spouse. "And I can't believe you would help a stranger without considering Diana's feelings."

Appealing to his wife, Nicky spread his hands awkwardly. "I didn't think it would matter since I had his agreement in writing. There is nothing he can do without Diana's consent." He turned back to the haven of his office with both women following close on his heels. "Here, look, Diana." He opened his safe and pulled out a small packet of papers. "Read it. Everything is spelled out. Even our lawyer said it was a superb deal." His eyes pleaded with her to understand. He avoided looking at Maggie for one moment. He had felt badly about not telling Diana, but keeping it from Maggie had almost ruined him. If he hadn't been offered such a great deal, and if he hadn't known how much Maggie silently ached to be free of the demands of running the rink singlehandedly, he would never have agreed.

Diana, with Maggie looking over her shoulder, scanned the document. Everything Nicky said was true. The question was why would a man reputed to be ruthless in all his dealings, both personally and professionally, offer such a one-sided deal. Confusion replaced her anger.

"I don't get it," Diana muttered.

"I don't either," Nicky admitted with a shrug, praying that the worst was over. "The funny thing is that he initiated the discussion of your time. I didn't have the chance."

Diana looked up at that, her frown deepening. It just didn't make sense. "You mean he had this ready for you when he approached you about buying this place?"

He nodded, risking a quick look at his wife. When she didn't glare back, he breathed a sigh of relief. "I mean just that. Maggie and I have been talking about selling, but I hadn't gotten as far as putting the rink up for sale."

Diana didn't find his words reassuring. "Then how did he know about it?"

"I don't know. Every time I asked him, he would get a look on his face that made me stop asking questions. I quit asking and just took his check, a check, I might add, which was half again as much as I had thought about asking."

"What are you and Maggie going to do without this place?" Diana asked abruptly, too surprised at the revelations to think clearly. "Travel?"

Nicky grinned, looking years younger than his fifty-four. "We might not be going anywhere. Starke wants us to stay on as long as we like. He's got big plans for this place and he's offered me the job of manager if I want it. I haven't given him my answer yet. I was waiting until the deal was completed before I told Maggie." He looked at his wife, his voice deepening. "I wanted to surprise you, honey."

Maggie studied his face, her expression confused but no longer angry. "You did that all right." She moved toward her husband. "I know how much this place means to you. I didn't think you would ever sell. I thought we were only talking. And a manager? You?"

"Us. He wants us both. It will mean more time off, less responsibility in the long run. We'll be able to do all those things that we haven't done and still stay here.'' He touched her cheek gently. ''It will mean the best of both worlds for us.''

Diana sat down in the chair facing Nicky's desk, hardly noticing the small reconciliation going on between Nicky and Maggie. She needed to think. She just couldn't get a handle on Jason's motives. Nothing that was happening seemed in character for the man she had spoken to last night, or the one whom the papers termed ruthless and cold. A competitor such as he had been wouldn't have paid a penny over the asking price of the rink. And she would be willing to bet that whoever his source had been on the potential sale had also known the price tag that would be put on the property.

''Have you seen these plans?'' she asked suddenly.

Nicky reluctantly released Maggie to sit down facing Diana. ''No.''

''Aren't you curious to know what you'll be getting into if you do agree to take the manager position?''

Nicky shrugged. ''I was. But Starke made it clear that he wouldn't have offered me the shot if he hadn't thought I could do it. Not only that, he said he was buying my name in a way and he also pointed out that if I didn't like what he was doing or didn't want to work any more, I would have the resources to take a walk. The man had a point. I don't think I would have been so blunt in his place, but I had to admire him for stating the facts up front.''

''I know the feeling,'' Diana admitted, her own

memories of Jason's strange brand of honesty extremely vivid.

"Forgive me?" Nicky asked carefully.

Diana sighed deeply, not sure what the future held but knowing that she could not hold Nicky responsible for the decisions he had made. He had done his best. It wasn't his fault Jason probably had some scheme up his sleeve that she didn't want to know about. "You know I will."

"I should have told you."

"The contract took away any danger to me. We both know that."

"At least you won't have to look for another rink."

"You mean I won't have to face not finding another rink of this caliber. Rink time is at a premium here."

"Well, I'm glad you know. Now, when Starke comes to town this week, you two can meet."

Diana managed to mask her surprise that Nicky didn't know Jason had already arrived. "When is he due in?"

"His secretary didn't say when she called yesterday. She just warned us he would be seeing us soon."

Diana got to her feet, more confused than ever. What had Jason hoped to gain by arriving unannounced. The sale was all but complete. She headed for the door with Nicky and Maggie following. "It will be interesting to see what changes the next few months bring," she murmured before taking her leave.

"They'll be for the better. Starke doesn't seem to be a man to start a project and not make a success of it. I'm really curious to find out what his plans are," Nicky added thoughtfully.

Jason rolled over and glanced out the window of his condo. The snow was falling heavier than it had been when he had awakened the first time two hours ago. He frowned at the white powder, not seeing it but rather the face of the woman he had come to find. Not having any picture except one of her as a long-legged teen, he hadn't been prepared for what ten years had done to her. Her skin was smooth, flawless ivory, with what he could swear was a natural rose blush to her cheeks. Her lashes, both upper and lower, were dark and extravagantly long. She moved with the grace of a ballerina and spoke, even when she was furious with him, in the most softly-modulated voice he had ever heard. She seemed to glide through his memory as she had floated over the ice last night. He had come prepared to offer her almost anything for her services and found that he could hardly recall his goal because of the clouding of his mind with emotions that were unfamiliar and male needs that were inopportune. He shifted uncomfortably, the imported cotton sheets caressing his naked body, making him fully aware that desire in an empty bed was as useless as udders on a bull. Annoyed with himself and the direction of his thoughts, he got up and paced to the window.

He had no doubt by now that Diana was meeting with Nicky or on her way there. In her place, he would have been furious at having had the rink sold out from under him. Knowing the relationship that existed between Nicky, his wife, and Diana, he figured it wouldn't be long before Diana got a look at the contract he had drawn up. He glanced at the clock on the bedside table and wondered if she would face him with the information or would she wait for him to bring the subject up. His lips curved slightly at the thought, although there was no humor in his eyes as he returned his attention to the landscape. His plans were moving along nicely. With the exception of his intense physical attraction to Diana, he had figured all the possibilities, including the variables, and had allowed for all contingencies. Now, all he had to do was wait for the next act to begin.

Diana glared at the blank sheet of paper in front of her and blocked out the soft rock music coming from her tape machine. It was no use. She had never sat this long trying to work out the initial stages of a routine and still come up empty. Usually, this was her favorite part of her work, the time when her enthusiasm for the new project was at its peak. Today, nothing she did seemed right or even mildly creative. She tossed down her pencil and popped up from the couch to turn off the tape.

Silence filled the house, but even that didn't satisfy her. She glared at the clock, wishing the hours away. Three more and Jason would arrive. Even now, she wasn't certain how she would handle herself. Even now, she didn't understand what he was up to and what tactics he would use to get her name on a contract for his complex. She didn't fool herself into thinking that he wouldn't push her harder than she had ever been pushed before. Without those bits of knowledge, she would be lost before she began. But how to ask? She couldn't just blurt out that she was feeling stalked, backed into a corner where the only way out was to throw her lot in with his. Was that what he intended? She didn't want to believe it, but she couldn't find any other explanation. The contract was some kind of key, but the reason eluded her. She just wasn't goal oriented enough, she decided, to have plans so far reaching that to look closely was to miss the point.

Jason guided the rental car down the narrow street leading to Diana's house. The snow had stopped falling, leaving the landscape a pristine white bathed in silver from the full moon. Tall silhouettes of the evergreens lining the road stood like sentinels guarding a modern-day castle. He smiled slightly at his suddenly poetic turn of mind as he pulled to a stop in Diana's drive. Light spilled gold out of the windows, welcoming anyone who would call. He wondered briefly if Diana realized her depth of warmth for others. Even now, as he sat in the silent car feeling the cold of the night seep past the artificial heat surrounding him, he remembered how good it had felt to be near her, to listen to her speak, to watch her eyes light with emotion. And her skating. All of the things he knew to be his weakness were perfection in her hands. She brought life to the music and the frozen arena that seemed to drain the essence from him every time he stepped onto the diamond-hard surface. He, who envied no one, envied Diana her open heart and mind to the true beauty of their sport.

Shaking his head over his own thoughts, he got out of the car. He was done with being a performing robot with only cold precision instead of passion to light his life. Even if he could not learn from Diana how to breathe fire into his skill, he would do his best to make certain no other skater had the same training that had killed his soul.

Diana heard his car. She glanced at her reflection one more time and decided that the scarlet sweater and black wool skirt were simple enough to go most places and restrained enough to handle almost any kind of evening. Until she understood Jason better, she wasn't about to allow him to come any closer. She hadn't missed the faint flickers of desire lighting the darkness of her solitary life. Passion without emotion would never work for her.

The doorbell rang. She moved to answer. His eyes were the first thing she sought when she opened the door. If there was a clue to be found of the real man, it would be there. Admiration, curiosity, appreciation, and caution. A strange combination, quickly masked with polite approval.

Disappointment washed over her as she stepped back. He had promised a truce. She had taken it to mean honesty between them.

"You are very punctual," she murmured when he didn't speak.

"Training. Habits hard to break." He unbuttoned his coat as he turned to face her. "You look lovely."

"The expected compliment."

His brows rose at the quick return. She was wary. Had she forgotten the truce? "But true."

"Maybe, but I'm not responsible for a gift of the mixture of genes that produced me. And you don't have to go through the motions of making the proper comments." She lifted her head, the light catching the dark fire of her hair. Her look challenged him.

He met her eyes, thinking, assessing, waiting. "You think I'm doing that."

His expression was pure Jason, calculating, cool, controlled. "You sound as if you are."

Jason frowned at that. "I didn't mean to."

She shrugged, wishing she had one ounce of his control even as she watched it splinter a little. Anger dug deep, almost as deep as her disappointment that the truce was only an illusion. Her lashes dropped as she sighed. She turned from him, not wanting the night to begin with a war. "I shouldn't have said anything." She glanced over her shoulder.

"But you did." He stepped closer, trying to understand her. If they were to build his complex, if he were to learn from her all that he needed, he had to know the way her mind worked. Logic went only so far when dealing with the human element. "Don't you think you owe me an explanation?" He watched her eyes flicker, uncertainty and confusion mixed.

"I don't know . . ." She turned back to him spreading her hands. "You sound so untouched by things. Doesn't anything bother you?"

"I lost my temper the other night."

"Barely, and then under extreme provocation."

He smiled slightly at her disgust. Once again, Diana found his smile touched some part of her that she would have preferred protected. The urge to run had never been stronger. He was getting to her. Not with desire or wanting, but with that smile. Then, he sobered and, for an instant almost too quickly gone to be measured, she saw an agony of which she wouldn't have believed him capable.

"I'm not an emotional person."

The bleakness of his reply dammed whatever response she might have made. She stared at him, seeing that invisible emptiness she had only sensed the night before. "Why?"

He could have refused to answer, but not while looking into her clear eyes demanding the truth of his soul. "People who are ruled by their emotions court disaster in the form of torn up lives and ruined relationships. I have never wanted, nor could afford the risks, so I channeled what little emotion I did have into my skating and you know just how little that is." The words poured from him as blood from a never-healed wound.

Diana heard a strange hint of yearning that she wouldn't have credited. "It bothers you." The look on his face warned her she was getting close to a truth he didn't want exposed. "What they say hurts you." His lips made a mockery of a smile and this time she wanted to hide from its brilliance.

"An Iceman can't be hurt."

Without thinking, her hand rose to touch him. He tensed, looking down at her delicate fingers on the dark fabric of his coat sleeve. "Pity, little soft heart. A mistake. I'll use it if I can." Even as he issued the warning, he breathed in the bite of emotion that had given it life. It was happening. He was feeling pain. He could have shouted for the joy of discovery even as he hurt.

She stepped nearer, drawn by something she didn't understand but couldn't deny. "I know. I see more than you think."

His eyes caught hers, probing the gentle strength he saw there. Curiosity slipped through. "You should be afraid."

"I am."

"I'm not gentle."

"I know that, too."

He wanted to shake off her hold, but couldn't bring himself to break the contact between them. "You're going to get hurt."

"Probably." Neither tried to pretend the conversation wasn't covering many levels.

Anger touched him, lightly at first as he looked

at her, seeing the caring in her eyes. "Are you into pain or something?" he demanded irritably.

"No. Like you, I survive the best way I can."

He stilled at the softly delivered response. "Meaning?"

"That contract. The purpose is too deep for me, but I'd be a fool if I didn't know that it's some kind of insurance."

"I can tear it up." He almost sighed with relief. For a moment, he had wondered if she realized his personal need for her rather than her expertise.

She shook her head. "You know that the quality of Nicky's rink time would be next to impossible to duplicate. Every rink in this city is booked solid with a waiting list longer than I am tall."

He lifted her hand from his sleeve and brought it to his lips in a gesture so alien to him that even he was amazed he would try it. "Maybe I wanted to insure that your talent wouldn't hit a snag because of me."

She smiled then, a sad curve of her lips to echo the knowledge in her eyes. "I don't think that was it."

Jason weighed his needs against hers and wished he had the courage to explain what his life had become and what he had turned into. He wished he were strong enough to risk rejection and even pain for the truth. But he couldn't. The scars of a lifetime couldn't be removed with just a wish. Bending his head so he would no longer have to look into those gently demanding, sad eyes, his lips touched her skin, lingering to caress the velvet flesh. "You have a vivid imagination."

She inhaled at the brief flash of agony in his eyes before his lashes dropped to shield his feelings from view. His kiss in her palm was butterfly soft and yet carried the power of the tail of a lash. She flinched, startled at the gesture, the words, and the eerie silence that suddenly surrounded them. It was as if the world had stilled, waiting.

Lifting a hand to his hair, she threaded her fingers through the strands. "Tell me about you," she whispered. "Help me to understand."

Slowly, drawn by her words, he lifted his head. The need to deny her was strong, but the will to give was more powerful. Without knowing it, a wall that had been years in the making crumbled to dust.

FOUR

Jason started slowly, his memories hazy with the passage of time. He told of his large family, his parents and their do-or-die philosophy; his gradual realization that he was nothing more than a body to be molded, fine-tuned, and then used to the last of his reserves. Then he began tracing the tale of disillusionment. "I was thirteen years old when I really learned not to trust the most honest looking people. I had already developed a rather lopsided way of looking at things because I had been in training since I turned seven and had a succession of tough taskmasters. I was a cynic even then, but I still had some illusions. Until the day I watched a coach fix a simple, preliminary track-and-field meet. This guy was an ordinary man whom the town thought was extraordinary in his devotion to the boys he coached. The stakes were a small medal, a bit of confidence for youngsters just starting to think about dedicating themselves to the excellence needed to go on to higher

things. The coach thought he had the perfect reason for his choices. The boy who should have won
the meet was out with a broken leg. Another kid,
one who was constantly second to the first one,
would have taken the prize and ultimately gone on
to study with my father, who was a coach in the
Olympic program. He owed my father a big favor
and the boy with the broken leg was my brother.
The coach deliberately sabotaged his own protégé
to make sure that one of the lesser contestants beat
him. The judges awarded the kid his medallion,
and because my father only took one of the top
two in his region in points, my brother got the
slot. The other kid ultimately made it with another
coach, someone with less experience. As you know,
that kind of thing can be very important in the
early stages.''

Diana watched his face as he recounted the past,
seeing a rainbow of emotion bound up in the short
story. ''Did your father find out about what
happened?''

He nodded abruptly, his face going blank. ''I
told him.''

''And?'' she prompted, wishing she had never
started the conversation. Something more than what
he had related so far was terribly wrong.

Jason hadn't thought about the incident in years,
hadn't wanted to think about it. His father had
been a hero until that time, someone he had tried
desperately to please and to emulate. ''My father,
a man who had preached honor and the Olympic
code to all of us since before we could talk, did

nothing. His answer was that Eugene was the best and my brother needed the best.'' He shrugged tensely. ''Then he added the best reason of all to the list. He wasn't the one who had set the fix up and he only had my word that it had occurred at all.''

Diana drew back, horrified at the disillusionment that Jason must have felt at the callous dismissal. Jason watched her face change, the knowledge in her eyes. Since he had begun, he might as well finish. ''I went back to training camp that same day and applied to live with one of the foster families that the kids from faraway used. My mother was upset and my father so angry that he never forgot what I did. I never lived at home again. All that stuff about honor and right was just so much hogwash when the chips were down. Once my eyes were open, I found a lot of things going on that, while not totally black, were so grey it was hard to tell the difference.''

''Not everyone is like that.'' She repeated the platitude that had been given her so often when her parents were alive and then later by Nicky.

His smile mocked her defense. ''Is this the woman who withdrew rather than continue to compete?''

''I didn't want that kind of one-dimensional life any more. That can't be all that hard to understand, and it certainly isn't the first time an athlete has quit.'' The lie started years before slipped from her tongue without thought.

Jason shook his head, his gaze focused on her

face. "The more I get to know you, the less I believe that load of trash the papers put out at the time. You don't act or react like a woman who couldn't take the demands of our life, and you certainly didn't get out of the business. I've got a fairly good idea of the hours you put in now and have for quite a number of years. The two just don't compute."

Diana froze, fighting to keep her expression blank. When would the past stop haunting her? Hadn't she paid in hell for the actions of others? Hadn't her word cost her the pain of journalist spies, avidly demanding questions, and numerous invasions of her privacy? Why couldn't people forget and let the past lie? "I was younger, more susceptible." Again, the stock answer came forth, only this time tinged with regret. Jason had trusted her with his truth. It seemed a betrayal not to give her own in return.

"Smarter. You had the courage to say the emperor was naked."

"I cut off my own nose and hurt a lot of people."

He stopped, surprised at the bitterness and regret in her response. "Would you do it differently if you had it to do all over again?"

Diana looked away for a moment, the question was one that she had asked herself a hundred times and still had no answer. At the time, her choice had seemed the only course for all concerned.

He stepped closer, his hand cupping her chin to bring her gaze back to his. "I've told you more than I have told anyone for a long time. Whatever it is, tell me. I won't use it ever, I promise.''

Her eyes widened at the vow. The temptation to share her experience was almost too strong to resist. The restrained plea in his eyes was draining her will. ''I never thought you would,'' she whispered.

Jason knew the moment Diana decided not to let him closer. The sting of rejection was harsh. Irritated that such a small thing could hurt so, he drew back, slamming the door on his feelings. ''Forget I said that. I told you not to trust me. That still goes. But I do want you for my project.''

Diana shivered at the steel-tough purpose in his eyes. ''You don't mean that,'' she whispered, suddenly knowing that this price was too high for a ten-year-old promise.

''Honey, how did you last this long? Of course, I mean it. I came here to find you. Don't tell me you're forgetting the contract already. I came prepared with just what I needed to win. You can't beat the terms of that contract and you know it. You've got a house here, and unless you are prepared to move or have enough money to build your own rink, I have you unofficially attached to the complex if no other way.''

Diana listened to the sharp summation and knew she had almost made a terrible mistake. For one moment, she had allowed herself to be taken in by Jason's softer side. For one moment, she had almost sold her honor to save him pain that he couldn't feel. "I had thought of that, but I had hoped I was wrong. You came here with the trap all set."

He inclined his head, his eyes never leaving hers. He read the disillusionment as clearly as if she had shouted it. Regret touched him, sinking in claws that tore at the fiber of his soul. He ignored the agony and kept his goal firmly in mind. "I didn't want it this way, but I'll take you any way I can get you. This is important to me. I've had this dream for a long time, and I've searched for just the right people to help me with it. I knew the odds were against your agreement, or even a fair hearing. I'm counting on your professionalism and the caliber of the staff I'm putting together to turn you in my favor in the end."

"I hate bullies," she blurted out, too angry to keep the words back. "All my life, until I had the courage to dig in my heels, I've been bent, pushed, and spindled by coaches, trainers, and public opinion. You can't force me to do something just because you want it. My life is in my hands. It's my decision whether I come or go." She jerked her head away from the warmth of his hand to walk deeper into the living room. Until this moment she hadn't noticed he still wore his coat and they had been standing just inside the door. "And more than that, our date is off. I don't want to look at you, much less talk to you again. You've got me cornered right now, but I'm going to do my best to get out of your trap." She turned to glare at him.

The emergence of the feelings tearing at him were making a mockery of his control. He had never blundered so badly in his life. Because he didn't have much else to lose, he pushed. "I would have thought you a woman of honor. You said you would go out with me."

"That was before I found out what you were up to."

"You just admitted that you suspected what I was doing."

If Diana had been a swearing woman, she would have had a few choice oaths. "You can't make me," she retaliated, knowing no other way to respond. The moment she said the words, she knew she'd made a mistake. His almost gentle smile caught her once again. "And quit smiling at me. I wouldn't put it past you to have practiced that little trick in front of a mirror."

He followed her into the living room, taking off his coat as he walked.

"What are you doing?" Diana demanded.

"What does it look like I'm doing?" he asked reasonably. He was back in command of himself and this time he would stay that way. Taking ill-advised walks down memory lane had a lot to answer for. It was time he started using his head.

"You aren't staying."

"I'm collecting on our date. I can't let you break your word. I don't want you regretting me in the morning." Diana, despite her words, was no more immune to him than he to her. He was counting on that to get him through this last debacle. He wouldn't use his appeal, but he was banking heavily on proximity to soften her determination. The one thing about emotional people was their inability to clamp down on their responses. That trait was their greatest strength and most blatant weakness.

Diana backed away as he drew near, but she could have saved herself the trouble because all he did was take a seat on the couch. "The only thing I regret is ever meeting you."

He chuckled at her disgusted mutter. "I bet you do. Although I can do a lot of things, unfortunately turning back the clock for either of us isn't on the list," he admitted, a wealth of self-mockery in the last few words.

Confused by his about-face, intrigued by the way he could put away their angry words as though they hadn't been spoken, Diana moved a step toward him. She wanted to hold onto her temper. She had a feeling that she was walking into a carefully baited trap, but she couldn't see where the cage was. "If you feel that way, why keep after me?"

"You know why, professionally." He shrugged, waiting, testing her nerve as he left the answer open to interpretation.

Diana sensed the trap. "I won't get involved with you personally."

"Do you think we have a choice? If it's any consolation to you, I don't understand you any better than you do me. Your ability to feel makes me uncomfortable and it brings out emotions I don't handle well. My life has been built on planning, cold facts, and logic. You don't seem to respond well to any of that." He hadn't expected her bluntness, and found he not only respected and admired her for it, but that it was just what he needed.

Diana felt oddly close to Jason. She didn't trust him fully, hardly understood him, and in general felt as though she were walking through a maze to which only he had the key. It was a dangerous feeling, made even more so by the excitement building within that demanded she try to reach the center before he did. "Then walk away."

He smiled grimly. "I will if you can. Look at us now." He waved a hand to indicate the close proximity of their bodies, despite the differences in position. "You should throw me out on my ear. Instead, you are listening to me even though I'm saying things you don't want to hear. I'm telling you more about myself than I would dare with anyone else. I'm trusting you."

"I think you are playing a deeper game than I can see."

He laughed aloud, pleased with her caution. "The only way you'll know for sure is to walk the game board with me. Watch my moves and see if you can win."

Oddly enough, for all her twenty-nine years, no one had ever challenged her mentally before. Diana stared into his eyes and knew that he had hit on the one argument that had any hope of holding her interest.

On seeing her curiosity, Jason finally relaxed. "You like that. I thought you would. Whether you admit it or not, you are a lot like me. Better perhaps in many ways, but tough and bold." He rose in one smooth motion. "You won't regret this. Take your place on the starting line. We begin even." He pushed one sleeve, jacket and shirt, up past his forearm. The corded muscles stood out in stark relief against the fabric. "No tricks up my sleeve. Whatever either of us can catch and hold, we keep. All things are wild and any strategy goes."

"You're crazy," she whispered, the challenge blotting out the last of her inhibitions.

"Determined, desperate. You take your choice." He leaned toward her, his lips inches from hers. He had come to learn the secrets of the professional who could fire the ice with her emotions. He had discovered a woman who demanded more of him than he thought he had to give. He had tried to hold back, fighting his need to warm himself in the blaze of her passions. Walking out of the rink into the snow and darkness had brought reality sharply into focus. He was turning into a frozen human landscape. He needed heat to thaw the ice before it was too late. The risk was terrible. The future was littered with traps he had no way of protecting himself against. A fire was one of nature's least controllable elements. He could get burned so badly that being frozen might be a blessing.

"Haven't you ever wanted to take an impossible gamble for the sheer hell of it?" His hands held her flesh as he sought to entice her mind. Her eyes were bright, eager, passionate.

"No." She licked her suddenly dry lips, mesmerized as much by his question as the desire glowing deep in the night-dark depths of his eyes. His smile denied her lie. "Yes," she breathed huskily, drawn to him as lightning to a single tree in the field.

Jason released his breath in a long sigh as his mouth closed over hers. He had waited too long to rush. His lips savored the satin texture of hers, nipping gently at the soft curves until she opened to him. Even then, he didn't plunge in. Rather, he teased her and himself until her tongue joined his in a delicious foreplay that awakened needs so intense his body went rigid in resistance. She yielded in his arms, her curves molding to his as though they had been formed together, then torn apart only to return to fuse once more. Her hands on his back were delicate, yet strong enough to bind him to her had he wanted to break away. The soft sounds coming from her throat touched him deeply as she responded to his caress.

Diana felt the body she had thought she knew so well change into a being she had never known. The feel of Jason against her brought heat and fire to melt a glacier. She had no defense against his power because she had gone into his arms unprepared for the force they generated. A flicker of fear called back her sanity, her caution.

"Tell me you can walk away from this," he whispered against her throat. He traced a line of kisses to her ear.

Diana shivered, this time from passion not cold. "I can't do this. How can it be like this?" Even as she denied him, her arms held him tighter. "We'll hurt each other."

"We'll survive."

"It isn't enough." Desperation drove her. She had known what it was to lose something so very important that rebuilding her world had been almost impossible. She couldn't do that again.

He raised his head, gauging the depth of her resistance. The look in her eyes stopped him as nothing else could have. Fear, stark and unrelieved, cooled the heat in his blood and brought out a strange need to protect, to shelter.

"I'll take it back," he groaned, hating what he was, not knowing how to change and wishing he could.

Feeling the fight he waged to let her go, Diana stilled. She searched his face, seeing the tension in his expression, the fierce need to take that he denied. Fear receded, leaving behind a curious kind of tenderness. She couldn't walk away from Jason. Whatever the future held, she had to reach out to him. "No, deal me in. I'll match you play for play."

He touched her cheek, his palm cradling the elegant curve. "I won't lie to you. If you ask and I don't answer, it's because I won't lie to you. Ever.''

"Honesty. I give it as well." She smiled slightly, strangely relaxed now that the rules were laid. "The novice and the master of games, tricks, and illusions. A strange combination. An upset in the making or a foregone conclusion?''

"Whatever. A combustible mixture.''

She tipped her head, already learning to look deeper for the clues. "You want the fire.''

He said nothing.

"You came here for more than the complex.''

Again he said nothing.

"I'll figure it out.''

"I hope you do,'' he said quietly, with more depth of feeling than anything but his desire for her had shown. "But I won't make it easy for you.'' He bent his head to take her lips once more. This time there was no gentleness, only a man's need for the woman he had chosen.

Diana responded as though there were no tomorrow. Tonight, a truce surrounded them. When he raised his head, they were both breathing heavily. Desire swirled in the silence, an invisible web to trap the unwary.

"Shall we stay here or go?'' Jason asked softly, his hands caressing her back in slow, soothing strokes.

"Go. It's safer.''

Jason found humor in her quick response. His eyes flickered, light entering the dark depths. "One thing I've discovered about you, you're never wishy-washy about what you want."

She laughed, enjoying his amusement as much as his passion. "I've learned to stand up for myself out of self-defense."

"You seem to have made it well." He knew it was time to release her, time to return to the cold that was his world when he wasn't touching her.

"Are we both going to try and get through my door this way?" Diana asked, wiggling gently for her freedom.

Jason glanced over his shoulder as though giving the matter thought. "The idea has appeal, but I think I'll save it until we know each other better." He dropped his hands slowly, savoring the warmth of her skin for one last moment. The memory lingered after he tucked his fists into his pockets.

Diana turned to get her coat, missing the confusion and the resignation in his eyes. "You never did tell me where we were going."

Jason followed her out onto the porch, waiting while she locked up. "I found a small restaurant near here. It's quiet and not loaded with a lot of people. The food is good."

"I know the place. It is good. But how did you know?"

"I asked a local." He opened the car door for her.

Diana got in, masking her surprise at the gesture. Jason was a study in contrasts. If she were to stay one jump ahead of him in this game between them, she had to learn the man and how he thought. Settling back, she vowed to do just that. She didn't understand the stakes, but her senses, developed to a fine edge in the dog-eat-dog world of competitive skating, told her more was at risk than just whether she accepted a position on his staff. Truce or no, she couldn't allow herself to be lulled into giving Jason an advantage, no matter how small. She had to stay alert, on guard. She glanced at him, seeing the expressionless mask that was so much a part of him. Her task wouldn't be easy. For one fleeting moment, Diana wondered if the risk was even worth the reward. What was it about him that demanded she walk blindly forward?

"You're thinking," Jason murmured without looking at her.

"Shouldn't I be?" Diana returned quickly.

"That's my forte. Yours is emotion and feeling."

"You say that as if one can't exist without the other."

"Perhaps they can't."

She considered the possibility. "I can see where you might think that," she conceded after a minute. "But I don't agree."

He glanced at her then. "Good."

Studying him, she demanded suspiciously, "I thought we were having a truce."

"Surely a little skirmishing is acceptable."

"Not without a good case of indigestion."

Her tart rejoinder caught him off guard and he laughed. "Meaning, I should feed you first before trying anything?"

"That depends on how you define *anything*."

He shook his head, delighted with her conversational volleying. He didn't know another woman, except his aunt, who would have crossed verbal swords with him. He liked the sensation even as he worked to win. "I define anything the way the dictionary does. How do you define it?"

"Within the context of the subject at hand."

"The rink? Or something else?"

"The rink is safe enough. We'll set the parameters there."

"And if I don't agree?"

"Then I don't play."

"I think I walked into that one."

Diana smiled slightly, then sobered. "Your answer."

He shook his head, knowing she was growing stronger with every cross of verbal swords. "You play hard."

"I had a good teacher."

Jason considered the situation. "All right. We'll settle the rink problem first. One way or another." He paused, trying to understand her. "I may regret this," he added, thinking of the plans he had laid, the strategy he had implemented, and the completion of his dream riding on the unpredictability of the human mind and heart.

"We may both regret this," she corrected, sighing and knowing that she would not draw back.

"I enjoyed dinner, but where are we going now?" Diana stared out the window, recognizing the route but hoping she was wrong. This was the way to Nicky's. The night was quiet around them, dark, mysterious, and yet beautiful with the silver-and-white landscape contrasting with the shadows of darkness. She wanted more than she could say to sit back and let the pleasure of the evening fill her senses.

"Nicky's." Jason didn't need to look at Diana to know she had tensed. He was taking a risk, but the easy rapport they had established at dinner had given him the idea. He wanted her to see with his eyes, if only for a moment.

"The truce is over, I take it."

"Not exactly." He glanced at her then, the next step in his plan was important. "You said you weren't ready to be officially involved with my complex, but that doesn't mean you can't unofficially look at the specs and give me your opinion."

Diana relaxed slightly, but remained alert. Jason was a master at turning inches into miles of gained ground. "I really like the way you've altered my words. A nice move."

Jason inclined his head. "I thought it rather adroit."

"Perhaps, but a tad unsubtle." Diana paused, letting the silence lengthen as she considered her options. Admitting that she didn't want to know what she was turning down was unthinkable; as was confessing that she was becoming interested in the few hints Jason had deliberately let drop over dinner. Better to let him think he had cornered her again, rather than let him know she was mulling over his offer. "We both know I'm biased against it from the start," she argued for appearances.

"All the better. There are too many people around me prepared to say yes simply because they feel I expect it. You won't do that." His eyes pinned her, demanding the truth.

Diana didn't hesitate. At least this she could answer with a clear conscience. "No, I won't do that."

He nodded, satisfied. "Then you'll see them."

"You think if I see what you'll be doing it will change my mind?"

"I wouldn't sell you that short," he denied immediately.

That pulled her up quick.

"A few lines on paper won't make you change your mind. It isn't the building you object to, but what you're afraid will go on inside that worries you. We both know the kind of people that inhabit professional sports. Most are dedicated, with a true love of the various skills. But there are always not so savory ones around, who simply use or misuse the talents of others. We have been on the receiving end of both kinds, and fought our way clear in our own fashion. The struggle left scars. Yours and mine. You handle yours by running from them. I deal with mine by trying to make a place where that kind of thing can't happen."

Diana inhaled at the unexpected thrust. His picture made her look selfish and him courageous enough to rise above his past. Irritated, but determined not to show it, she replied, "I don't run."

He ignored the bite in her voice. "What do you call it, then?"

"Choosing not to participate in something I don't believe in any longer."

He was quick. "Semantics."

She was, too. The game was escalating. "Honesty."

"You should have been a lawyer." Jason pulled into an empty slot in Nicky's parking lot and got out of the car.

"Instead, I'm only the choreographer you want," Diana murmured, nodding to the security guard as they passed through the lobby to the rink. They stopped at the door of a small office in the back. "I'll see your plans because, in a way, you are right. I have been a coward. I'll do my best to be honest."

He touched her cheek, guessing what her concession must have cost. "That's all I ask. Selfish was a low blow, but I needed you to think. To hear me."

Diana looked into his eyes, waiting, wondering why he kept sharing his tactics with her. A game within a game, or a man trying to find his balance in the confusion that surrounded her? She wanted to trust him, but without the answer to that question she couldn't. "I only promise to try," she murmured.

His smile touched her gently. Diana felt the warmth. And she had thought him cold. He stepped back and gestured her down the hall. Diana walked beside him, wishing he hadn't touched her, and yet curiously wishing that his hand was still sharing his warmth with her skin.

back and gestured her away the rink. Diana wished she could find anything to equal to Jason's rapture, watching Nicky skate, but there was still another role waiting to be filled.

FIVE

Conscious of Jason's quiet presence in the silent office, Diana studied the plans of the buildings Jason intended adding on the empty land around Nicky's rink. The layout was almost the equivalent of a college campus in design. What she had envisioned as a small training camp took on a new dimension. She raised her eyes to where Jason stood watching intently from the shadows.

"Are you financing all of this yourself?" The plans were too extensive for one man's fortune.

He shook his head. "There are five of us all together."

"Professional skaters?"

"All but two. The others are really money men."

She glanced at the list of prospective staff, hopefuls eager to attend the new facility, and various other personnel that would be required behind the scenes—cooks, gardeners, trainers, cleaning people, and so on.

"I had no idea you meant something this big."

Jason pushed away from the wall to join her at the desk. "You're the first one outside the group to see the total plan."

Her eyes widened in surprise. "Won't they mind?"

"It doesn't matter. It's my dream and I hold the controlling interest."

In anyone else, Diana would have found arrogance in his statement. In Jason, it was simply an assessment of fact. "Why Denver? There are other rinks. Other cities. You come from Minnesota. Why not there?"

"I wanted it to be here."

She looked down at the plans. His reply didn't invite any more probing. Once again, she had stumbled into an area where he would give her only so many answers. Her temper stirred, but she banked it. She wouldn't move him that way. Her anger would roll right off him.

"It's impressive," she murmured finally, her admiration reluctant but real.

"Do you like it?"

Had she not been listening so carefully, she would have missed the need for her approval in his voice. "Yes. It has everything."

"Still not tempted to join us?"

She lifted her head, expecting at least a flicker of triumph and finding only a guarded watchfulness.

"I'd be lying if I said I wasn't. You have some of the most sought-after names in the business on this roster, people I admire and respect."

"But?"

"I've seen things happen to plans that start out great and end up less than adequate."

"Don't forget to add that we're skaters, not business people," he finished for her.

She nodded. "You have to admit the possibility of problems on any number of fronts is there."

"And if I promise that nothing will go wrong?"

"No one could promise that."

"I can. I do."

"How? You've been on the circuit since you turned pro. Are you hiring someone to run this for you, beyond Nicky, I mean?"

"I've been retired for two years. And I'm going to be heading this up. I intend to settle here."

Diana leaned a hip against the edge of the desk, studying him as he looked at her. Every one of his answers was short, to the point. None betrayed more than the information she asked. Every sense sharpened as Diana tried to pierce the brevity of his replies for the plans she felt lay beneath. "You settle here? Why?"

"It would be rather hard to commute if I didn't."

A non-answer. She wondered why as she filed the evasion in the back of her mind. "Let's skip that and get to your qualifications for running a setup like this. Where did you learn, if you did learn, that is? If you had been doing anything like this, the media would have reported book, line, and verse."

His lips twisted at the mention of his faithful followers. "If I had let them know what I was up to, perhaps."

She said nothing, only waited.

"I have a degree in business administration. I've spent the last two years as an apprentice to a very influential man, one of our investors, actually. I won't pretend that I learned everything there is to know about corporate life, but I learned enough for my teacher to decide I had a good shot at making this work. He had enough faith in my abilities to throw his weight into helping the group I formed to get the other money men we needed."

Jason's determination and discipline were awesome. She couldn't even begin to comprehend the kind of dedication his course had taken. "Maybe I should agree now and save myself the trouble of losing," she murmured, wondering if she really had a chance in this game they played.

"Conceding me the victory?" He tensed, knowing he couldn't be this close, this soon. He didn't want to win this easily.

She shook her head, every instinct crying out against surrendering now. "No. NO!" she added even more strongly.

He relaxed with a soundless sigh. "You're too much of a fighter to let me win by default."

"You didn't think that earlier."

"I am wrong occasionally, very occasionally," he said dryly as he rolled the plans into their protective cylinder for storage. He followed Diana to the door and out into the hall. "Now, what? Do you practice tonight?"

"Yes. I really should be getting home. I have a bit of paperwork for the program to get set before I can work on it on the ice.'' She glanced at her watch. Practice would provide an uncontrived, but necessary, break from Jason's presence. She needed time to come to grips with what was happening between them.

"All right. I want to come with you tonight. Will it bother you if I watch?'' He opened the car door for her, catching a glimpse of surprise in her eyes.

Diana hesitated, startled that the thought of having Jason watch her produced none of the fear she expected. Was it possible she was finally beginning to lose that paralyzing terror of being in front of a critical audience? "Why?'' She could argue the first time Jason had caught her unaware and then later angered her so much she had forgotten her past. She had no such excuse now.

"I like watching you skate.'' A partial truth, but she wouldn't know that.

"I'm used to the late hours.''

He smiled slightly. "And I'm not?'' His brows rose at the flimsy evasion.

Diana flushed faintly, something she hadn't done since she was a teenager. "Stupid comment. As I recall, the compulsory figures could be held at the most unusual times.''

"Don't forget the pro shows. Some of those lasted late and after costume changes and so forth, I put in a lot of late hours.'' He closed her door and went around to his side. "So, what will it be? I return to my lonely condo and you to an empty rink, or we share the night together?''

In the close confines of the car, Diana felt the heat of his body and the strength of his will wrap around her as though together they could command her agreement. Her heart speeded up its rhythm, her breathing quickened, and her lips tingled as she stared at him in the semidarkness. Although he wasn't touching her, she could almost feel his arms about her, her body softening to his. His eyes flickered, desire beginning to glow so brightly she found herself leaning nearer. A spell. An enchantment. She had to break the silence, the invisible ties with which he was binding her more securely with each passing second. She jerked back, licking her dry lips as she shook her head.

"Stop it," she commanded huskily, cursing mentally at the inviting throb she could not subdue.

Jason raised his hands, palms up. "I haven't done anything."

Diana hesitated, wanting to deny his claim, but knowing if she did she would open more of a Pandora's box than she could cope with at the moment. "All right. You may come."

Before she could protest, Jason took her lips, lightly brushing the soft curves. "I promise I'll behave," he murmured as he raised his head.

She stared at him, wanting to believe him and knowing she shouldn't trust him an inch. "I notice you didn't say how you would behave," she whispered.

He smiled at her, again delighted that she was so quick. "So I didn't, pretty lady." This time his kiss settled on her forehead, light, delicate, and infinitely tender. Feeling more content with his world than he had in a long time, Jason started the car.

Diana leaned back in her seat, gazing at his smile. What was it about the simple act that caught her attention? How could one change of expression do so much for his austere features, turning him from a man with frozen emotions into a male with unlimited capacity to respond? Which was the real Jason? And more importantly, how safe was it to try and discover the truth?

Jason sat on the bench waiting for Diana's music to begin. On the way back to the rink, she had explained about the professional skater for whom she was creating the routine. His eyes traced her movements as Diana went to the center of the rink and lifted her arms, preparing for the opening. As he looked on, he saw Diana's personality disappear and Melinda's emerge. The melody began. Diana's head lifted, tossing, her eyes flashing wickedly in the first showy leap. Diana's natural skill was subdued, chained by the limits of another skater's talent. The moves were beautiful, eye-catching, and so totally lacking in the tremendous depth Diana brought to life on the ice that Jason felt cheated before half the routine was complete. Stirring restlessly, he glanced down at the skates he had brought in while Diana had changed into her workout clothes.

What would she say if she knew how he longed

to join her on the ice? Would Diana be able to see what he needed from her? He reached for the case, opening it to reveal the gleaming silver blades of his favorite skates. Without thinking, for the first time in his life only feeling, he drew them out and slipped out of his shoes. With practiced ease, he tied the laces and rose to his feet. If he hadn't been obeying an impulse, he would have been in more suitable clothes. The black slacks to match his pullover sweater wasn't ideal attire, but it would have to do.

The music swelled, reaching the apex of sound that demanded an exquisite aerial. Instead, Diana, as Melinda, settled into a blur spin. It was then his control broke. He opened the door to the wall separating the rink and seats and glided onto the ice. He knew the moment Diana sensed his presence. He saw her falter, her eyes questioning. Then he touched her. His hands settling on her waist.

"Dance with me," he commanded.

"You're crazy."

Both knew that couples spent years working together to perfect the timing needed for two to skate in synchronization. Partners had to develop the ability to give each other complete trust. The blades on the skates were just that—blades—sharp, deadly in their capacity to cut and slice. One wrong move and disaster could strike without warning.

And yet, as they stared into each other's eyes, it

was as though this moment had been ordained from the instant of meeting. Diana slipped into a simple glide, waltz step. Jason followed, feeling the tremendous smoothness of her stride. Although shorter than he, she had a long reach, making his work all that much easier because he didn't have to shorten his stroke by much to accommodate hers.

"Turn," she said softly, leaning slightly to the left.

Understanding at once, he responded by reversing direction. They circled the rink, neither listening to the music while they learned each other.

"Will you trust me to throw you for a jump?" he asked as they stroked side by side, becoming more attuned by the second.

Diana didn't hesitate. Whatever questions she had about the man, on the ice she knew she could not be in better hands. "Yes."

He smiled, a strange exhilaration filling him. His hands encircled her waist. He lifted her, watching her eyes as his arms extended full length. There was no fear, even as he threw her out and away, spinning across the unforgiving surface as though she had conquered gravity and all its mystery.

Diana held his gaze as she dropped, her arms positioned gracefully to echo the double twist she executed. She landed without a bobble and his smile became hers. The tape finished, but neither noticed as they came together at the center of the ice.

Jason wrapped his arms around her, caging her now like he hadn't done in reality. "You are superb. You shine more brightly than the sun." Once again, he raised her high overhead, holding her suspended above him. "I want you more than I have ever wanted anything or anyone in my life. Will you give yourself to me the way you gave your safety into my keeping just now?"

Diana looked down at his intense face, reading the desperate hunger he made no effort to hide. "I hardly know you."

"True, before this moment."

"Skating is different."

"Only in that it demands the best in us to give or we fail." The strain of holding her above him was beginning to tell in the muscles of his arms, but still he kept her aloft. "Answer me. No evasions. Truth."

"I need time."

"Why?"

"To know you." She felt the fine quiver that ran through his arms. "Put me down before you hurt yourself."

"I notice you didn't say before I drop you."

"It didn't occur to me." The quiver intensified. "Let me down."

"Answer me."

"All right," she breathed, giving in because she realized he would not. "But this is blackmail."

He brought her down, easing her body over his before he set her on her skates. Every muscle in him hurt for one reason or another. Holding her above him, and himself back from taking what he needed, was stealing his strength.

"Never that, my snow queen. See what is happening to us?"

"I see insanity in all ways. We don't match. You scare me and make me feel as though I could fly to the sun. I trust you here, but step off the ice and I watch everything you do suspecting a trick." Her fingers flexed into the muscles of his shoulders as she tried to fathom his reasoning.

"It is no better for me."

"What would happen if I agreed to join you in your complex?"

"Between us?"

She nodded, watching him, searching his face for something to give her the answers she sought.

"Nothing would change, except that we would spend more time together. I would still want you. In spite of what you think about what happened just a few minutes ago, I won't take your freedom of choice from you. I want you so badly I feel as though I am on a rack with some mad torturer. But I won't take what isn't given freely. I am not built for half measures. I will neither give you pieces of myself, nor will I accept only pieces of you."

"So, it's all or nothing?"

His eyes narrowed, the dark irises deepening to black. "Isn't that always the way when something of real value is at stake?" Now that he was beginning to understand how important Diana could be to him, he was no longer willing to learn a few of her secrets. He wanted them all. He wanted to tame the fire to his hand and yet leave it free to burn as bright or brighter than ever.

As a conversation stopper, Jason's remark couldn't have been better. Diana risked holding his hot glance for one more moment before she allowed her lashes to close, blotting out his face. His will against hers. The contest was both more simple and more complex than she had thought.

Jason felt the tension invade her body and knew it was time to back off. He had given her enough to think about for now. "You're tired. Let me take you home." He brushed her hair back from her forehead, disliking the paleness of her skin. He had not meant to frighten her. Damning his own stupidity, not to mention needs, he brought her close to his body. She resisted for a minute until she realized he only wanted to hold her. When he lifted her in his arms, she laid her head on his shoulder.

"I should never have gone out with you," she murmured, wondering why she was letting him carry her when she had been ready to fight only seconds before.

"It was inevitable."

"Your victory?"

"No. Perhaps my defeat."

"Are you trying to make me feel better?"

He sat with her in his lap. "No. You don't need my sympathy. If you only knew it, it is I who need yours." He grinned at her startled expression. "Now, sit still so I can get your skates off."

"I don't need you to do that." Diana wiggled around, trying to reach the laces he had already begun untying.

"Keep that up and I'll think you are ready for me."

She stilled immediately, her breath emerging in a long, thoroughly annoyed gasp. "What I would like to be is free of you."

"We both know that isn't true." He pulled off the first skate and focused on the second. "But, if it makes you feel safer, tell yourself that. It won't matter in the end."

"You remind me of water on stone."

"I've been called worse." He released her foot and tucked her skates into their case.

"By friends or enemies?"

He laughed. "Both. Although I have more of the second than of the first."

Diana flinched at the matter-of-fact way he summarized his life. "That can't be true?"

He shrugged, too accustomed to the situation to care. "You know the kind of competition that exists in our business. And you also know the kind of nonexistent social life we have. Why so surprised?"

"Don't you have anyone who loves you?" Had she been thinking clearly, instead of just responding, Diana never would have asked the question.

Jason sobered. "Two people. And one who has my respect," he added on reflection.

"Women?" she guessed, suddenly angry that

there could be someone in his life while he touched her with desire in his eyes.

He caught the flash of jealousy, finding that he liked her possessiveness. "Two are. Lorelei. And Pippa."

"Lovers?" she demanded, startled at the faint depth of emotion in his tone.

"No. Sister. Aunt. In that order, and before you remember the other and start firing up, he's Lorelei's new husband. A tough man who sees my sister as the sun and moon of his universe."

Diana let his words sink into her heart, finding fertile ground to grow. So, Jason was capable of some kind of affection for others, although admittedly in small quantities. The papers had been wrong. He wasn't an iceman at all. Even now, when he could have been seducing her, he was taking care of her, talking to her, giving her clues to his life and his thoughts.

"Where do they live?" she asked, more curious if he would reply, than any need to know about the people.

"Georgia. A little town called Tyrell to be specific. Alex has a country place there to get away from the pressures of his computer business in Atlanta. My aunt's is the only house close by. She's a writer and Lorelei stayed with her while she recuperated from an accident. That's when Lorelei met Alex. And gave him the devil's own time convincing her to marry him."

Not expecting that much information, Diana listened so intently she got caught up in the story.

Jason was different when he spoke of those who were important to him. His eyes were softer, deeper, his voice gentler, more reminiscent. "Why did he have trouble?"

Jason shook off the memories to look at her, reading the very real interest in her expression. "Lorelei was in a serious auto wreck. Her legs were damaged severely; at one point her doctors thought she would never walk again."

Diana inhaled sharply. "How terrible!"

"That wasn't the worst of it. She had been a gymnast of the caliber of your potential in skating before you quit. She was a year away from her first bid for the gold. She lost her career and . . ." He paused, his muscles tightening as he remembered the devastation his sister had gone through at the time.

Diana read the pain in his face all too easily. The knowledge that it had been her curiosity that had brought him to this hurt. "But there is a happy ending for her, crippled or not."

Imprisoned between the past and present, Jason's temper fired at the words. Too many people— his family, Lorelei's so-called friends, and teammates—had labeled his sister a cripple. "Don't use that word. You don't know anything about the situation. Lorelei isn't crippled. She has a limp and a few scars, but she isn't crippled. She rides like an Amazon and gives parties that everyone fights to get invited to. Alex is a high-powered man in a cutthroat business, and she matches him step for step.'' He rose, almost dumping Diana on the floor.

Diana's balance was due more to her superb conditioning than intent. She moved a pace away and planted her hands on her hips, suddenly as angry as he. ''I meant no criticism of your sister. Frankly, I admire her. I don't know what I would have done in her place. I chose to quit my field. I didn't have it snatched from me just as I was on the verge of attaining all that I had studied and sweated blood to reach. As for Alex, I think that without even knowing him I like him. It takes a special man to look below the surface to the person beneath. I'm glad they got together in the end.'' By the time she finished, she was all but shouting, her breath coming in hard pants of temper. How could he think her capable of such insensitivity?

''And furthermore, I don't thank you for believing I would think less of your sister because of a physical problem that was neither her fault nor something she could do anything about.'' Glaring, she bent and lifted her skate case, wishing very much she had the nerve to sling it at his head. ''Now, I am going home. Suddenly, I find I don't like your company at all,'' she stated vehemently. Without looking at him again, she turned and headed for the door, prepared to walk if she had to in order to get away from him.

Jason watched her go, tracing her rigid spine with regret. He hadn't meant to insult her, hadn't even thought of how she would react. He deserved her anger, but he also knew he was getting fallout from a different kind of anger altogether. He had pushed too hard and too fast. Cursing his ineptitude, he started after her. Now, he had to retrace his steps again and hopefully undue the damage.

SIX

"Wait!" Jason commanded, reaching for her arm.

Diana swung around, in no mood for anything except a ride home. "Why? So you can hurl some more insults my way?"

Jason held onto his temper with effort. "Don't you think you're overreacting a bit?" he asked, striving for a calm tone when all he really wanted to do was shake her silent.

"I do not." She was, but she wasn't about to admit it despite the skeptical look in Jason's eyes.

"Supposing I apologize?"

She studied him. She could almost feel the waves of frustration pouring off him. "Are you?"

"You're pushing."

"And you haven't been?"

He opened his mouth, paused then rephrased what he had been about to say. "Probably."

"Definitely." She tried to hold onto her anger but found it slipping from her grasp.

"Being with you, talking about my past—my life—is hard for me."

"I can tell. So why do you do it?"

"I need to."

Now Jason had her full attention. "Explain."

It was his turn to step back, putting distance between them. "Not now. I need to think about it." Jason turned slightly from her, knowing she deserved more of an explanation and yet incapable of giving one right now. "I'm trying to work some things out. This complex is only part of it," he said, still watching the darkness surrounding the rink rather than her. Her silence drew his glance. "I want to give you more."

Diana studied him as much as the limited light would allow. So few words at such a great cost. She could feel the effort he had made to tell her even this much. She wondered at the whole and knew she would not ask. She, too, had secrets that she could not share. "We're a pair, you and I," she murmured sadly.

Her hurt went through him, slashing through his needs until only hers mattered. He had hardly touched her and yet he had caused her pain. He couldn't live with that. "Let me get these skates off and then we'll go. I'll take you home as you wanted in the first place. Forget the complex and me." He urged her back toward the bench where his case waited.

Diana planted her feet. "No way. Whatever we may or may not be to each other, I'm not running this time and I won't let you, either. You barged into my life. Not the other way round. You're staying put and seeing this through."

Jason took her arm, refusing to release her even though she tried to shake him off. "Look what I have already done to you."

"I'm a big girl now. I can take it, if you can," she retaliated, getting angry all over again. The coldness that had cloaked him the first moment they met was back in full force.

Jason glanced at her with icy eyes. "Damn, I'm trying to protect you, can't you see that?" he shouted in frustration.

"No. I see a man trying to protect himself."

He turned from her, dropping onto the bench and snatching at the laces of his skates. Diana looked at his downbent head and wished she had the key to his thoughts. But more than that, she was as baffled by her own behavior as Jason seemed to be. Neither spoke as he collected his case and escorted her to the car. The drive home passed without a word.

Jason stared out at the night sky, watching it lighten slowly as dawn crept closer. He should have known better. Diana was a curious, intelligent woman. How long would it be before she began to look for a reason for his determination to have her involved with him on any level he could get? His fist balled as he fought the urge to slam his hand into something painfully hard. Emotions. He had wanted them and denied them for so long that he was in danger of losing what little grasp he still had on humanity. The events that had driven him out of the skating arena and into private life were only one part of his past. Every day he was confronted with even more of his own inadequacies. The phone shrilled in the silence, startling him into a harsh oath. He turned, glaring at it. Only the hope or fear that it might be Diana compelled him to answer.

"Well, it took you long enough," Pippa grumbled.

Jason sat down on the edge of the bed and stifled a sigh. He could have almost predicted he would hear from his eccentric aunt. "What do you want or did you call just to harass me?"

Pippa's ever-ready antenna picked up the disturbance in Jason's tone. She frowned faintly, knowing her instinct had not played her false. Jason needed her. "You know better. I'm in the middle of a book and your name keeps getting in my way. What are you up to?" she explained and demanded in a spate of choppy words delivered in a husky voice that could and probably had driven more than one man crazy with wanting. "The last I saw of you, you were on your way to Denver, hopefully to find the key to your own prison. So, tell me, how is it going?"

"It's not." Only with Pippa did he have trust enough to voice his doubts out loud.

On the other end of the line, Pippa's frown deepened. She started leafing through her Rolodex for the number of her travel agent. There were exactly three people in the world who could pry her away from a good plot. Jason was the first of the trio and, on the surface, the least likely to need her help.

"Are you going to explain or do I need to drag it out of you?"

"I blew it."

Pippa was never one to mince words. "How? The Jason I know has too much finesse and liking for the females to mess up."

"Well, I did. In spades. I pushed when I should have held back. I've told more partial truths than even I can keep up with and the topper to this little trash heap of stupidities is that I insulted her badly right after I forced her into admitting she wanted me." This time his curse wasn't as lurid as it had been when he was alone, but it was no less vehement.

"You are in trouble. I warned you that your idea might blow up in your face. You have closed yourself off for a long time. Opening up to the world of passions, wants, and needs is a road that can be hell."

"Tell me something I don't know," he returned with unexpected bitterness.

Pippa ignored the ill-tempered rebuttal. Her eyes gleamed as she found the number she sought. A smile that Jason would have recognized and distrusted on sight curved her lips. "Why don't you sit back for a few days. Let the waters calm for you and her. By then, something is sure to pop up to turn the tide."

He groaned at the advice. "You would think a

writer with your vivid imagination would come up with something better than murdered cliches. Besides, I'm not good at sitting." He rose to pace restlessly.

"You'd better learn before you wreck everything beyond mending," she responded tartly.

"I don't see what sitting on my a . . . rear will do."

"You'd be surprised. Now, hang up and let me get back to work. You go play with your complex or something, and let your lady alone for a while."

Diana took off her skates while glancing carefully around the empty rink. It had been two days since she had last seen Jason. Courtesy of Nicky, she knew his plans for the skating project were speeding up. Also courtesy of Nicky, she knew that Jason was at the rink for hours each day, sometimes working in his tiny office, at others meeting with contractors and architects. But she hadn't had a glimpse of him. It was as though he had stepped off the edge of the world as far as she was concerned. And yet, while the newspapers were full of his plans for the complex, there hadn't been one mention of anything of a personal nature. No pictures, no gossipy tidbits.

Diana couldn't understand it. Even when he had retired from the professional ranks, Jason had still gotten coverage. What was going on? And more importantly, why did she care? Why did his image follow her to sleep each night and awaken with her every morning? Why did she have trouble concentrating and why was it getting harder not to peer around corners hoping to see him?

Jason faded deeper into the shadows as he watched Diana get into her car to leave. For two nights, he had been an invisible escort to the parking lot. For two nights, he had endured the steadily increasing need to speak to her. Only Pippa's advice had kept him silent, waiting for . . .

He turned away, disgusted, frustrated, and not certain what he wanted anymore. Everything had seemed so simple when he had envisioned his plans. The complex was going well. The sale of Nicky's was complete and ground would be broken for the new buildings as soon as the weather cleared. He drove to his condo, knowing that the time of waiting was over. Right or not, he was going to have one more shot at putting his relationship with Diana on track. He parked in the driveway, glancing idly at the townhouse he had decided to purchase. The lights burning in the windows came as a surprise. The figure standing silhouetted in the doorway was a shock. As usual, his unpredictable relative was where she shouldn't be, probably contemplating meddling in his life and wearing another of her outlandish, designed-to-get-her-arrested outfits. The woman followed no rules except her own, and tread where even he would not dare.

"What are you doing here?" he demanded, stalking up the stairs to his own door.

Pippa grinned, not in the least put out by his

irritable tone. "I'm the cavalry, honey. To the rescue and into the breech, and all of that." She patted his cheek, while lifting her own for his kiss.

He glared at her for all of a second while she stood poised before him with that cat-with-a-belly-full-of-canary smile which he disliked heartily. "You are not staying here," he muttered, giving her a kiss. Despite his best efforts, her exertion on his behalf, no matter how misguided, touched him deeply.

"Actually, I would much rather be at home digging into my story, but with you intruding in my thoughts that's out. So, for my own sake, not yours, I hopped on a plane. Lorelei was devastated, of course."

Jason grinned, feeling oddly less tense. "I bet. She's probably hoping whatever I've gotten into will keep you busy for a while," he shot back, mocking her affectionately.

Pippa tossed back her head, laughing at the idea. "Most likely, but she's really too nice to say so. Unlike you, my sharp-tongued devil of a nephew, she's blind to my manipulating because she loves me. You see me as I am and react accordingly. I need that." She shrugged gracefully, almost losing possession of the off-the-shoulder, oversized silk top she sort of wore.

Jason barely noticed the delicious display of femininity. Pippa's bizarre, often just barely decent clothing amused more than scandalized—as it did the rest of his relatives—him.

"You're trying to change the subject. I can

always tell. You may fool the rest of the relatives into thinking you're harmless, but I know better,'' he warned, watching her closely. "Just why did you come?''

Pippa sobered, her bright eyes shrewd and kind at the same time. "To help. When you first told me what you were intending, I was worried. Both for you and the woman you believed could help you. But I listened because I know you have an animal instinct for what is best for you. You believe that being around and with Diana will help you to unlock yourself and your skating. I'm all for that. I don't like what you've become any more than you do. You need Diana's fire. I watched those tapes you left at my house, those ones from when she used to compete. I see what you mean. I understand, but I don't know if you do.''

"Pippa, more than anyone else, I care about you. But I won't let you interfere.''

Pippa faced him, her expression both gentle and determined. "Then it's a good thing you can't stop me, isn't it.'' She wandered deeper into the living room to take a seat on the chocolate leather couch. The blouse slipped even lower. Neither noticed. "I've watched you grow up. Self-centered as I am, I could still see you turn into yourself as you fought the pressure being brought to bear on you. I watched the playfulness die before you turned six. I saw the disillusionment when your brother got that place in your father's school because of a fluke loss that wasn't a fluke at all. I've watched you claw your way to the top, and I've watched you turn off all emotions until even the critics could see the lack in your skating.''

Jason shifted restlessly, wanting to stem her words and yet unable to bring himself to stop her.

"I watched you the night you won that last championship. The night your so-called best friend was injured in that freak mishap. He was your biggest competition that year. That reporter who interviewed you right after the win even asked you how you felt about his injuries, and how you thought it would have come out if the two of you had gone head to head.''

"I stood in front of that camera and said I would have won. I was at the top of my form and it was my last year. Sounded like an arrogant fool,'' he said quietly, looking beyond her to the past he had tried to leave behind.

She nodded, not sparing him but not condemning him either. "I know why you quit.''

That got his attention. "I told everyone why. I wanted to go out at the top of my form.''

She shook her head. "Good press, but not the truth. You were beginning to see what skating and the search for perfection that had been drummed into your head before you were old enough to make your own choices had cost you. At a guess, I would say you woke up one morning and realized you couldn't feel anything, or maybe so little that there wasn't much difference.''

He wanted to deny her assessment, but couldn't. "Maybe.''

Pippa's eyes narrowed at the studied, offhand

tone. "It's strange how much little things can mean in our lives. Take, for instance, your father's funeral. You couldn't attend because of that competition in Europe."

He stiffened at the reference, but kept silent. He knew better than to try to stop Pippa when she was on a mental track.

"You didn't know he was hospitalized. He wouldn't let anyone tell you because he wanted that championship for you. I don't want to even think how I would have felt in your place at being denied those last moments with someone who had had such an important place in my life."

"I understood why he did it and there was nothing I could have done, anyway. So don't think I am or was feeling guilty."

"And the funeral?"

"What about it?"

"I'm the one who called you, remember? You didn't even hesitate to refuse to fly home." There was no condemnation in her voice. Pippa, like Jason, realized the sacrifices that had been made.

"He wouldn't have wanted me to quit in the middle of the contest."

"But that wasn't the reason, was it?"

Jason turned away from her to pace to the window. The night was fading fast. Another day. "What do you want me to say?"

"The truth. You need it. You can't survive without it."

"I don't know what you're talking about."

Pippa rose and pulled him around to face her.

"Listen to yourself. Someone else would be angry at my prying. Not you. You don't get hurt, tired, or angry."

His lips twisted in grim remembrance. "Oh, I get angry all right."

Her brows rose in surprise. "I don't believe it. Who was the cause? Diana?"

"Yes. I told you, I messed up. My plans are blown right out of the water. I've all but told her what I'm doing here."

For once, Pippa didn't have a quick comeback. "No wonder you sounded as if you had been run over by a truck when I called you. You and your plans are inseparable. You never miss a trick or foul up."

Jason shrugged irritably. "Well, I have now. I've probably even made up for all the times when nothing went wrong."

Pippa grinned at the sudden sting in his words. "Hot dog!"

Jason shook off her hold and moved to the couch to throw himself down on the cushions. "Get that gleam out of your eyes. Just because you were instrumental in helping Alex and Lorelei, doesn't mean that I will welcome your expertise in my direction. In the first place, I came after Diana for professional reasons. She has more passion in the rink than I have ever seen. You saw her work. Even as a fledgling star, she could melt the ice beneath her skates. Since she has turned choreographer, every skater privileged enough to have her create a program for them is touched by that same fire. That's why I have followed her career all these years, and why I am pursuing her now."

"Mule muffins," Pippa retorted inelegantly. "Lie to yourself if you like, but don't try to snow me. Besides, this Diana sounds just like the kind of woman that you need to melt a little of the glacier that surrounds your heart. I can't wait to meet her."

"You aren't going to meet her."

Pippa wasn't fooled by the casual announcement. "And who is going to stop me? The last I heard, this was a free country."

Jason sighed deeply, feeling every one of his thirty-three years. "Don't do this. Go home and work on your book. I'm big enough and tough enough to take care of my own life. I'm not Lorelei and you aren't the good fairy who grants all wishes."

Pippa took the cushion next to him and laid her hand on his arm. "Let me help. You know I can. You said you had botched this up. At least tell me how. Maybe I can help you get that much straightened out."

"You can't." He covered her fingers in a comforting gesture rare to him. "I let my libido drown out my need for Diana's expertise as a figure skater. I went too fast and got slapped down for my stupidity. I'll eat crow and try a different tack. If that doesn't work, I'll look around for someone else."

Pippa frowned at the flat response. In all the years she and Jason had shared, she had not heard that tone directed at her—only at others. "It's that easy?" she probed.

"Why shouldn't it be? Remember I am a glacier. The Iceman." He laughed grimly, his eyes as bleak and unwelcoming as the heart of a blizzard.

Studying him for a long moment, Pippa made her decision. With or without his cooperation, Jason would have her help. "Can I stay for just a week now that I am here?"

It was Jason's turn to search her face. "You won't interfere?"

Pippa breathed a mental sigh of relief at the wording. "No."

He relaxed slightly, not aware until that moment that he had been worried. "All right. Even longer if you like. In fact, I'll take you skiing as soon as I can get a spare minute." He patted her hand and leaned forward to kiss her cheek. Having Pippa around would help take his mind off a certain woman who demanded more of him than he dared give. His insanity was over. He would stick to the original plan and forget the fantasy he had almost believed when he had held Diana in his arms.

"You'll like the shops here, especially the ski boutiques. I guarantee you can find something to please even your outrageous need for barely-there clothes."

"You know me so well. Alex teases me about my wardrobe, too." She glanced down at the scarlet and purple top and harem pants she was sort of wearing. "He even promised me bail money if I ever got arrested."

With every word, Jason found his world steadying, his control slipping back into place. He laughed shortly, tucking Diana back into the corner of his mind that had been hers for so long. "I knew I liked that man."

"He reminds me of you."

"He's better than I am," he returned instantly.

"Only in your opinion." Pippa slipped gracefully to her feet and sauntered toward the door leading to the hall. "I'm for bed. These late nights or early mornings, depending on your point of view, are not my favorite times of day."

Jason got up, still smiling. "By the way, I like the outfit. Very eye-catching."

Her saucy, entirely too wicked smile was the last thing Jason saw as she left him alone.

"Are you lost? Can I help you?"

Pippa turned slowly at the soft, solicitous voice. Her eyes made one quick, comprehensive sweep of the woman Jason had come so far to find. She was a beauty, there was no doubt about that. But it was the expressions that moved so fluidly across her face that were the real attraction. Her eyes were bright, clear but ever changing. Pippa felt her warmth even in the short moment of first meeting. "I wish you would," she admitted ruefully. "I'm usually quite good with directions and I know my nephew is better than average, but I can't make heads nor tails of this map he drew me." She handed over the slip of paper she had spent twenty minutes doctoring and looked totally befuddled.

Diana frowned at the strange scrawl of lines. This was a map? "Where were you trying to go?"

"Downtown."

"You won't get there from here." Diana glanced at the small compact parked at the curb. "Couldn't you tell you were getting into a more residential area?"

"I could, but I had told Jay to fix me up with a route that would let me see a little of Denver on the way in to shop. I'm only going to be here a week and I'd like to cram as much as possible into each day I've got." She frowned and peered at her map, hoping she had gotten the lines she had altered the same thickness and strength that characterized Jason's rendition. She didn't want to blow her cover at the first hurdle.

"I tell you what. Let me do a little changing on your map so you can get back on track," Diana offered, somehow liking the stranger in front of her. She looked like something out of a fairy tale with her long, silver-blond hair hanging down her back and the slightly wistful look in her incredibly blue eyes. Of course, the pale lavender pantsuit she had on contributed to the delicate, almost fragile image.

"Would you?" Pippa almost choked on the helpless tone, but managed it for Jason's sake. So, this was the one who brought fire to warm a frozen heart. She definitely approved. There was power and courage in that face. Beauty, yet it wasn't the first thing that struck one on seeing Diana Diamond. This was a woman who had come through the gates of hell and had emerged stronger and more clear-sighted than most. There was passion trapped in those eyes and barely contained energy coursing through a lovely, supple body. If Pippa had searched the world for a mate for her most-loved of relatives, she couldn't have found one better suited for her intense, driven-by-his-own demons Jason.

She watched for a moment as Diana bent to her task. "Is there a pay phone around here?"

Pippa knew very well she was in front of Diana's house. The remainder of the gas she had so carefully drained from the full tank of the rental car had taken her to Diana's door. Being a believer in signs, Pippa was even more certain she had chosen the right course in pumping Jason for Diana's schedule. Finding out she took a walk almost every day about this time had made her plan to create an accidental meeting a piece of cake.

"Is there a problem?" Diana asked, lifting her head at this new wrinkle.

Pippa worked at a dismayed expression, when she really felt like leaping into the air and clicking her heels together at her success. "I'm afraid I ran out of gas."

Diana laughed gently. "Don't worry about it. That's my house. You can call from there and share a cup of something warm with me while you wait, if you like."

"I'd like that very much. You've been very kind to a klutzy stranger." Pippa held out her hand. "My name's Phillippa, better known as Pippa to all but my enemies."

"Diana Diamond." Diana returned the gesture, liking the firm handshake she received. "Let's get inside and start solving your problem."

SEVEN

"I think that's fascinating. When did you decide that you wanted to choreograph as opposed to turning pro?" Pippa discreetly watched Diana, easily understanding how difficult Jason would find it just being in the same room with her. Every emotion was reflected in Diana's eyes, every tone of her voice traced the highs and lows of her feelings. Jason would have no defense against this kind of honesty, nor did he have the kind of insensitivity to take what he needed from one so vulnerable and seemingly without defense.

Diana shrugged before taking a sip of her peppermint tea. She and Pippa had spent the last few minutes getting acquainted. Diana was amazed at how quickly the other woman had made her feel at ease, almost as though she were talking to a new friend. "I didn't exactly make a conscious decision." Pippa's question was a logical one given the circumstances. She had to be careful how she answered. "It was more of an accident than any-

125

thing else. I hadn't really expected the deluge of publicity when I retired from competition. It was a bit like drowning with everyone watching. I needed time away from skating to decide what to do with my life. My parents have a cabin up in the mountains. I went there. After days of solitude . . .''

She paused briefly, recalling how long it had been before she was well enough to even notice where she was in more than a vague way. Those days were moments she would never forget as long as she lived. Putting the pieces back together again had seemed almost an impossible task. But she couldn't say that. No one knew what the past had cost and no one ever would.

''. . . I needed a diversion and the only thing to be found was some classical music on the stereo. I started doodling around with a few moves. It wasn't long before I had a really good routine created on paper. I thought it was a fluke.'' More than that, she had thought herself a glutton for punishment for even considering taking to the ice again while her body was so run down, so lacking in the strength she had come to expect.

''I tried another piece and it wasn't quite as good, but I could see the promise. But more than that, I felt like something inside of me just clicked.'' Diana compressed the evolution of months of recuperation, failure, and despair into one small sentence. When she had discovered she could no longer face critics or groups of people watching her perform, she had been devastated, cut adrift from the only world she had ever known.

It had been her mother who had seen a way for her to stay with the sport she still loved. "Rather a strange way to begin, isn't it?" She made herself smile.

Pippa read more than she was certain Diana wanted her to see. She hadn't been wrong. This was a woman who had been intimately acquainted with pain and come through the experience stronger than ever. Because Diana expected it and the role she played demanded it, Pippa returned Diana's smile and an abridged confidence of her own. "Not really. That's how I knew writing was for me. All the planning and working isn't as satisfying as that moment when you know that something has snapped into place. There is a completeness to it that nothing else can touch."

"I couldn't believe it when you told me you are a writer. I've never met one before." She could have added that nothing about Pippa indicated anything more than a lovely woman pampered and protected from whatever blows life aimed her way.

Pippa grinned, deciding to subtly drop the helpless act in favor of her real personality. Diana was made for honesty and she preferred truth to lies. More than that, she had a feeling she could trust Diana with even the most sensitive of information. "We're not the alien beings that most of the public would think us."

"It sounds so glamorous, but I guess it's like everything else. It's only glitz on the outside and sweat and guts on the inside."

Pippa chuckled, liking Diana more with each

minute spent in her company. Her perception was a bonus. "I couldn't have put it better myself." The sound of a truck pulling into the driveway alerted the women to the arrival of the service station man with Pippa's gas. "It looks as if my stay is about to end." She didn't have to fake her regret.

Diana rose to answer the door. Now that it was time for Pippa to leave, Diana found she wanted her to stay. The afternoon had been pleasant, relaxing. "I don't suppose you'd like to join me for an early dinner?" she asked on impulse.

Pippa pretended to consider. Her timing had been planned to the last second. For one moment, she regretted having to trick Diana, but she stifled the thought with the knowledge she was trying to help Jason and that in the end would benefit Diana. "I have a better idea. Why don't you join me and my nephew?"

"I couldn't." Diana opened the door and indicated Pippa's car to the man waiting, can in hand, for directions. She turned when she was finished and picked up the conversation. "Your nephew might not like having an extra guest tossed at him. Besides, I have to work later."

"Nothing bothers my nephew."

"Oh, one of those," Diana murmured before she thought.

Pippa's brows rose at the wealth of feeling in the comment. "You have one of those strong-jawed types in your life?"

"Not exactly," Diana admitted, surprised to

find she had no trouble discussing Jason with this woman. "I thought at one time I might, but we had a little blow up over something so trivial I'd swear he wanted us to fight. He brought me home and I haven't seen him since." She frowned at the feeling of regret that still lingered. She had spent so little time with Jason that he should have been easy to forget.

"He's probably angry with himself for letting a tiny problem escalate into something big," Pippa murmured.

Diana shook her head, her eyes mirroring more loss than she knew. "Not him. I don't think he has enough emotion to create that kind of reaction."

Pippa stiffened slightly, just containing her need to defend Jason. "That sounds rather harsh from a woman I wouldn't have characterized as judgmental."

Diana grimaced, annoyed at her quick tongue. "Maybe it's just pique talking."

"Is it?" she asked bluntly.

Diana sat down, studying Pippa's face, seeing purpose and shrewd intelligence in eyes she had thought calm and slightly vague. "You're different. You even speak differently than when you came in, more decisive." Suddenly, something clicked in her mind. "Pippa." Twice in a few days she had heard that name. "I wonder just what the odds are that that nickname is commonplace enough for me to have heard it before, especially recently. And a nephew named Jay." Angered at another example of Jason's manipulations, Diana snapped,

"I don't know why I didn't see it before." Now that she connected Jason and Pippa in her mind, she could see a faint resemblance in their faces. Their coloring was totally opposite, but the expression in their eyes was close. Jason's were harder than Pippa's, less forgiving but no less shrewd. She couldn't believe she had been so stupid as to be taken in. "What is it with you Starkes? Is it something in your gene pool that demands you play games with people's lives? Or are your own so boring that you can't resist stirring up trouble for others."

Pippa looked beneath Diana's anger for the emotions driving it. In her own way, Pippa was as volatile as Diana. Only the need was too great to allow for her temper. "In the first place, I'm not a Starke. Jason's mother is my sister. It's bad enough I have to claim her; don't stick me with the personality traits of Jason's father, who was the epitome of self-righteousness," she replied abruptly.

Diana stared at her, stunned at the response. "You aren't even sorry, are you?" There was no remorse in Pippa's eyes or in her voice.

"No. And if you knew what was at stake and were in my position, you wouldn't be either."

"Don't bet on it." Diana got to her feet to pace the room. Nothing made sense. She should be showing Pippa to the door and yet she was letting her stay.

Pippa watched her, her belief in this woman's place in Jason's life growing.

"Did he send you?" Diana demanded, swinging around.

"It's about time you asked that. That would have been my first question."

"That's because you and he seem to be more up on the protocol of this kind of thing than I am," Diana replied. "You didn't answer me. Did he send you?"

Pippa laughed, genuinely amused at the thought. "Hardly. When he finds out that I sabotaged his map and drained the gas tank to strand myself here, he's liable to ship me back to Georgia stuck between the pages of my last book."

Reluctantly fascinated at the lengths Pippa had gone just to stage a meeting, Diana said, "Then, what are you doing here? And how did you know about me, anyway?"

Pippa sobered, studying Diana. "I knew because Jason discussed his plans with me for the complex and you before he came here. He needs you, your expertise and your name for his center." Pippa sighed deeply. "How could such a simple thing end up so complicated? You and Jason seem to be at cross-purposes. I know my nephew. He won't give up. He's spent his life tackling and overcoming obstacles that would have sent most people running for cover. He says you are the best. Are you?"

Diana laughed shortly at the blunt demand. "How would I know. And even if I did, I wouldn't admit it unless I wanted to sound like an arrogant fool."

"That's one of the differences between you and

Jason. He would have said he was the best in his time. Arrogant or not, he would have given the truth without pretense. That kind of honesty costs. Jason learned how to protect himself almost before he could read. He taught himself how to arrange his world, to get what he needs without depending on others, because those around him tried to use each goal he set as a way to tempt him into doing what they wanted. It's his built-in survival instinct. You spent part of your life in his world, in the structure where wishes are held like carrots before a donkey. Perform with brilliance or no reward.''

Diana didn't want to soften, but there was no escaping the truth. For her own sake, she had to remember the price she paid every time Jason got close. "Is that how he rationalizes his manipulation of people? Protection? Rather convenient, wouldn't you say?"

Pippa gave her a straight look. "You aren't a bitter woman, but you certainly sound it right now. What did Jason do that was so terrible? He couldn't have taken you to bed or he wouldn't be in such a foul mood. Besides, one-night flings aren't his speed when something or someone is this important to him."

Diana's eyes flashed. "I don't know what it is with either of you, but the end does not justify the means in my book. I don't like being maneuvered, being lied to, or evaded; and I definitely don't like people who sneak into my life without being honest about why and how they got there."

Pippa lifted her head, staring down her nose at Diana. "That was a rather blanket condemnation. Just where have you been hurt—other than your pride? Jason is hurting a lot more than that, and you're the cause. I want to help him. And now that I have met you, whether you believe it or not, you, too. I have spent the last two days in a whirl of activity just to move my tail from Georgia to here. Jason didn't call me. He wouldn't even if he were dying. He doesn't believe that he has a right to demand anything of anyone. But I love him. There are six years between us. I won't insult you further by trying to tell you he is like a brother. Thank God, I was only cursed or blessed, if you prefer, with one sister. Jason matters to me just as his sister Lorelei does. They are very special people born into a home that saw nothing but their extraordinary physical prowess. Both of them will carry to their graves the scars of what that talent cost them. Neither, without very special people in their lives, can be complete because the damage was and is too great. Lorelei found her mate in Alex. He understands the woman she is. But Jason is still alone, hurting and growing more isolated by the day. This complex is a chance for him to reach out to others." She rose to her full height, determined to secure this opportunity for Jason, if nothing else came of a relationship between Diana and her nephew. "I am going to do my best to make you listen to him."

"I have listened," Diana retorted. "It will be a wonderful place, but there are others along the same lines where kids are groomed to enter the sports arena on the whim of a panel of international judges. I can't be a part of that. I know the cost. As with Jason, I paid the prices until the tags were too high.''

Diana jammed her hands in her pockets, trying to calm herself and knowing it was a lost cause. ''When I had the courage to say 'enough,' the press hunted for some deep, dark reason for my retirement. Some of their conjectures were ludicrous and easily laughed away. Others were more lurid, ranging from I was pregnant with a Russian skater's baby, to I was dying from some incurable disease. My family and I were hounded like criminals. It was a nightmare that didn't quit for nearly two years. Even now, there could be some dog-nosed reporter who has time on his hands and decides to be the one to solve the great mystery of my exit.'' Finally, her temper was easing its grip. Weariness from defending herself over a decision made long ago took its place.

''If I throw my name in with Jason, all that garbage will be dragged up again. Jason, retired or not, is hot news. I think he goes out of his way to give the media something to talk about.''

''As long as they think they know what he's up to, they leave him alone.''

Startled at the unorthodox view, Diana paused.

Pippa smiled grimly. ''Jason is probably more rabid about his privacy than you. You're right, he goes out of his way to give the newshounds and gossip mongers a story. Then, while they have their noses buried in the carcass, he disappears.''

"The women?'' The moment the question left her lips, Diana knew she had made a serious tactical error.

Pippa pounced with the agility of a cat. "I thought you said you weren't interested in him that way.''

"I'm not,'' Diana denied vehemently, feeling stupid for even making the attempt to camouflage her curiosity. "But if I were to join Jason's staff, I wouldn't want some female trying to scratch my eyes out when my mind is on business.''

"Honey, you almost convince me. You've got sincerity down to the last nuance.''

This time the sympathetic look in Pippa's eyes and the sudden gentleness in her voice broke through Diana's resistance. "All right, stupid as it sounds, I do care.''

Rubbing her hands together as a witch would over her caldron, Pippa settled into her chair. "Good. Now, the first thing to do is make sure that Jason doesn't know how you feel.'' She eyed Diana's figure, ignoring her startled expression. "We don't need to do anything about your clothes. The colors are great and the style is right up to the mark. Having a place of your own is a decided plus, especially one as homey as this. Jason doesn't realize it, but he's a pushover for soft, cuddly furniture and fireplaces. Thank God, you have both.''

Torn between amusement and a first-class case

of exasperation, Diana sank into her chair to gaze at Pippa in awe. "Are you by any chance intending to play matchmaker?" she asked, too battered by too many emotions to put an ounce of feeling into her question.

"Well, of course, I am. You don't think I would give up an entire three chapters to come all this way to plead a business decision, do you?" she retorted indignantly, completely contradicting her earlier reasoning and totally unworried at the prospect. "Jason wouldn't have needed much help with that in any case. If you had continued to refuse, he had someone else he could call. In fact, the experience might have done his ego some good," she added reflectively.

There were moments in every woman's life when she has to surrender gracefully to the inevitable, or risk a hurt too great to be borne. One was childbirth, another the first time with a man, and this one, perhaps a once-in-a-lifetime experience, when one man so touches a woman that she finds passion laced so liberally with the fear of losing herself that instinct dictates fight or flee.

Diana was a fighter. She had learned the price of running was too high for her to pay. "All right. This time I don't intend to be manipulated by you Starkes, without at least having some say in the situation," she stated, wondering if human chess was a contagious disease or a simple case of mass insanity. This was her whole life she was putting on the line.

Pippa accepted her agreement without any indication that she expected anything else. "He wants you, you know."

"He told me."

"Your answer?"

Embarrassment was impossible with the kindness that was in Pippa's expression. "I agreed and he took off for the hills over the argument I told you about."

"Sounds like my blockheaded nephew. His ability to fool himself is equal only to his ability to bamboozle others."

"Bamboozle?" Diana queried faintly.

Pippa waved away the word. "You know what I mean." She frowned, staring off into space. "The thing is, he never goes into anything unprepared. He's probably figured out all sorts of contingency plans."

The phone rang, startling both women. Pippa let go a small shriek, followed by an earthy curse as Diana got up to answer it.

"Hello, Jason," she murmured, struggling to conceal her surprise.

Pippa joined Diana, pulling the receiver from Diana's ear, she held it halfway between them so both could hear.

"I wondered if you thought any more about my offer."

"Tell him no," Pippa mouthed.

Diana repeated the response, her brows raised curiously. She wasn't sure she should allow Pippa to get involved, but on the other hand, she wasn't certain she could have stopped the older woman if she tried.

Jason sighed, having expected nothing less. "I have a meeting with the architects today. You might be interested in hearing what they're planning firsthand."

Pippa grinned delightedly.

Diana didn't need another silent prompt to know what to do. "When?"

"Four. You'll come?" He had expected an argument, if not an outright refusal.

She ignored the question. "Where shall I meet you?"

"I could pick you up."

Pippa nodded vigorously. Diana ignored the gesture. She might be reentering the game, but this time she intended to have a few advantages on her side. "I'd rather not depend on you for my transportation."

Jason inhaled sharply at the barb he hadn't counted on, although he should have known a woman with Diana's passions wouldn't have allowed his behavior to go unmarked. "I should have started this call with an apology."

Feeling her way, Diana said, "It would have been nice. Especially if it was meant and wasn't one more move on your part."

Pippa's face filled with disbelief and dawning respect as she listened.

"It is meant. I've acted like a fool."

"In what way?" She was pushing, but she wanted a clearer picture of what she was up against.

"For crowding you, both professionally and personally. Somehow, I had the two tied up in my mind." He couldn't remember a time when he had attempted explaining his actions to anyone.

"And now?"

"You want your pound of flesh."

"I want to know where I stand before I put myself on the firing line again," she retorted bluntly, beginning to see distinct advantages in the Starke way of doing things.

"What are you asking for? My promise to leave you alone?"

"Would you give it?"

"No."

"I didn't think so."

Surprised, he paused, then asked, "Where do we go now?"

"That's up to you. Where we won't go is down the same path as before. I won't be dropped as if I don't matter, just because you aren't getting your own way."

"Fair enough. Anything else?"

"Complete honesty. No reservations this time."

He hesitated.

"If I ask a question, I want an answer, not silence, if you don't like what I need to know."

Jason thought carefully, not liking putting this much power in anyone's hands.

"The price too high?" She risked goading him, for an instant the confusion of emotions driving her getting the upper hand.

Challenged, he walked into the trap he had once

set for her. Even as he knew he was caught, he couldn't help admiring her nerve. "All right. Honesty, at all costs. I expect the same in return."

"You'll have it," she said promptly, mentally reserving only one place where she could not keep her promise. She hung up the phone, knowing this time the rules were in her favor, the strength in her corner, and the reins in her hands. She intended to keep it that way.

"I could have saved myself the trouble of coming here. You seem to know just how to handle Jason," Pippa murmured.

Diana glanced at the woman who had gone from stranger to cautiously handled friend in one afternoon. "I'm learning."

Jason stared at the phone, wondering what had happened. One minute he'd had hold of the conversation, and the next Diana had him agreeing to something that was likely to get him into trouble. But on the up side, he had her agreement to meet with the architects. Seeing the vision he and his friends were putting together in model form, if not in reality, was to know the potential of his plans. He was banking on her past experiences to have some of the same effect as his own. He wanted her with him, damn it. She had to see how valuable she would be to the whole. He stirred restlessly as his body reminded him of a few other reasons why he wanted her close. He ignored his responses as best he could, frustrated he couldn't cage the desiring beast that uncoiled within every time he saw or heard Diana. He had come looking for her passion, the depth of emotion she brought to the ice. He had hoped to warm himself for a time at her fire and then discovered that the fire was, in truth, a bonfire that would burn him alive if he got too near.

So, he had retreated, reevaluating his needs and the risks of reaching for them. Much as his body shouted for a mating with hers, he would not give in to the demand. He was the ruler of his existence. No one, nothing made that claim. Passion be damned. He had other plans. A woman was a woman. He frowned at the phone number of the very attractive flight attendant he had met on the plane to Colorado. The problem was, his mind knew one thing and his body another. It wanted Diana and no other substitute would do. Glaring at the mental image of her that danced teasingly out of reach, he balled up the paper and tossed it in the waste can. So, he would practice celibacy. The change might be good for him. Abstinence was supposed to build character or some such rot.

_____ EIGHT _____

Diana guided her car through the snowplowed streets, her mind on the coming meeting, Jason, and his unusual aunt. Oddly, she had forgiven Pippa her initial deception on the grounds of her clear affection for Jason. As for Jason, she didn't know what she wanted. She had tasted desire before, found it sweet, but with enough bitterness to make her cautious in her relationships. She led with her heart, often seeing costs too late to save her pain. Jason touched her. Denying it wouldn't change the facts. She had caught glimpses of the man he could have been before he learned to guard himself so well. She liked that man and wanted to know him better. But strangely, it was the master of evasion and trickery who intrigued and called to her more. She sensed within him a depth of passion to match her own. She had felt it stirring for those precious moments when he had danced with her on the ice.

His plans for the skating center were no longer

an issue between them. She knew she had held a grudge over the mistakes of a few glory seekers too long. It was time to step out of the past and walk into the future. Jason's complex offered her an opportunity to make a difference. She pulled to a stop in front of the architect's office, seeing Jason's car in a slot three over from hers. She watched as Jason got out and walked toward her. She tensed, not prepared for a private meeting, but not about to let him see that.

"I'm glad you came," Jason said as he reached her.

Diana slipped out of the car. "I said I would." Her voice surprised her with its steadiness.

He cupped her elbow, his fingers squeezing lightly through the thickness of her coat. "Let's not start one of our round-robin dialogues. Can't we pretend we have just met and nothing but a mutual desire to build something special is between us?"

Surprised at the carefully neutral plea, Diana stopped. She turned to search Jason's expression. The control was there, but also there was a faint glimmer of yearning. The walls were crumbling, not in an earthquake of rubble, but in a subtle shift of bits. "Is that possible?"

He searched her eyes, wanting to believe she had come to listen with an open mind and heart. "Anything is possible if you want it badly enough." He found an agreement in the faint relaxation of tension in her body. His breath eased out in a soundless sigh. He had felt the fool waiting for her in the car, but he had wanted this chance to put things on an easy footing if it were possible. It was time to end the mistakes he had made and get back to his original plan. His smile came slowly, lighting the harsh lines of his face, stealing years of experience and discipline frorom his expression.

Diana caught her breath and forgot all the reasons she had to be careful. This was the man she had touched so briefly on the ice, this was the man she looked for in her dreams, and this was the man who destroyed her ability to block herself off, in all except carefully chosen instances, from the sport she loved.

For a long moment their eyes held, each testing, probing for the truth in the other. Then, as though a mutual decision had been reached on some plane not verbal, they turned and continued up the walk, Jason's hand still touching her.

Jason entered his condo, humming under his breath. The scent of burnt offerings assailed his nostrils, denting but not destroying his mood. "I don't want to know what you burned, Pippa. Just tell me if you've made reservations for us at a decent restaurant," he said aloud, heading directly for the kitchen. As expected, Pippa was standing amidst chaos, a scene straight out of a cartoon strip. Pans and pots, probably every one he owned, marched drunkenly across the counters. The stove was smoking, blobs of charred foods creating miniature smoke signals, and more odors than a skunk could claim. The dishwasher stood open, haphazardly loaded, and the sink was buried under a variety of dish towels, more than likely all sporting at least one hole.

"Believe it or not, I was doing well until the phone rang," Pippa explained, propping her flour-covered hands on her hips. She had been, too. It had taken over an hour to create just this kind of mess without actually cooking.

"I don't believe it. There isn't one person who knows you at all, who doesn't know what a disaster you are in the kitchen." He glared at the mess. "This is your handiwork, so don't expect me to be a gentleman and offer to clean up."

"But you have to."

He shook his head. "No way," he stated firmly, on his way out of the kitchen.

Pippa followed him, bracing herself to draw her surprise out of her verbal hat. "You don't want Diana to see it like this, do you?"

He stopped in mid-stride, whirled around so quickly only his quick reflexes saved his balance. His eyes narrowed at Pippa's mischievous look. "I know I am going to regret this, but what do you mean? How did you . . . no, make that where did you meet Diana? And what do you mean here?" Visions of the progress he had made with Diana danced a wild jig in his mind.

Pippa cocked her head, judging his temper at halfway. She still had some maneuvering room. "Which question would you like answered first?"

His growl was more the muted roar of a lion whose tail had been jerked. Pippa decided she needed to reevaluate her judgment. "I met her because I ran out of gas and she was nice enough to get me to a phone.''

''Where did you run out of gas?'' he demanded ominously, memories of tales of Lorelei's problems with Pippa's meddling turning his brain to green mush.

''Does it matter?'' Pippa retraced her steps to the kitchen and decided that cleaning up was definitely a good evasion. She picked up a stack of dirty lids and started sticking them in the dishwasher.

Jason snatched them out of her hands and filled the machine himself. ''Answer me, Phillippa.''

''I know I'm in trouble. You're using my full name.''

''Can the theatrics. What have you been up to?''

There was no arguing with that tone. She sighed deeply. Why was it her relatives were so set against her help? She really was good at fixing things, the kitchen notwithstanding. ''I know you when you get an idea in your head. You go after what you want full speed ahead. Those tactics would repel the woman you described to me. I went to mend your fences.''

He glared at her, stunned into immobility at the announcement. ''You mean, you were there when I called today?'' Every sense rebelled at the thought Diana had come because of Pippa's pleading his case, rather than by her own choice.

She nodded, wincing at his curse. ''But I had nothing to do with her agreement, if that's what you're thinking. Frankly, I would have advised her to hold off. Judging from your mood when you came in, I gather that she agreed to join the staff.''

A diversion was called for if she wanted to emerge with her skin intact.

"Are you telling me the truth?''

She faced him squarely, not in the least disturbed by the question. "This time, I am. My word.''

He relaxed slightly, expelling his breath in a long-suffering whoosh. "That still doesn't explain what you meant about Diana coming here.''

"I called and invited her to dinner as a repayment for helping me. She accepted.''

Jason didn't know what to think. Despite the ease that had slowly built between them as they and the architect had discussed the plans, Jason had been conscious of Diana's careful avoidance of anything personal in her look or actions. Having made his own decision, he had found her attitude a relief. Why would she risk meeting him now on his home ground? It didn't make sense, unless by some chance she didn't know Pippa and he were related. But she did know the address. Maybe she hadn't remembered. He pinned Pippa with a look.

"Does she know you're my aunt?''

"She did before I left, but not at first,'' Pippa admitted, deciding the whole truth was an intelligent move under the circumstances.

"What do you mean at first?'' he demanded ominously. "What tricks are you playing?''

Pippa tried to look innocent. The expression would have worked with everyone but Jason. "Only a little one." If she had judged Jason right, his protective instincts should be cutting in right now.

Jason glared at his aunt, mentally consigning her to Hades forever. "You are worse than the plague. I told you how difficult the situation was. I asked you not to get involved. But did you listen?" His hands bunched into fists at his sides.

Pippa watched the changes in him with fascination. This was her controlled Jason! She felt like shouting for joy. He was furious. If she hadn't seen it with her own eyes, she wouldn't have believed it.

"Pippa, so help me, if you don't stay out of this, I'm going to wring your neck. And if you've hurt Diana or upset her in any way, I may do it anyway. This is my plan. Much as I care about you, don't help." He was breathing hard when he finished, but he meant every word.

Pippa touched his arm, feeling the rigidity of emotions held barely in check. "I care about you, too, Jason, or I wouldn't have tried." She smiled sadly. "You know, in all our years of helping each other, whether we wanted it or not, neither of us has ever been brave enough to risk putting that into words. Diana has been good for both of us."

Jason stared into her eyes, recognizing the truth in what she said. His anger died. "I wanted to," he admitted roughly.

She nodded. "Me, too. It's hard to reach out." She looked down at her hand. "I can't give you my promise, Jay. I don't lie, not like that anyway. I have to stay. And I will help if I can. But I will never hurt. Not you nor her. I would care for your sake alone, but I like her and I agree. She's had enough pain to last a lifetime. She'll have no more from me." She looked up, praying he would understand.

Jason searched her face. "All right, Pip. But don't expect me not to shout. I seem to be feeling like doing that a lot lately."

She grinned, more relieved than she would have admitted. "You wanted to feel again. Don't start squawking because you don't like the success of your plan."

A few miles away, Diana was asking herself why she had agreed to this dinner. When Pippa had called with her invitation, she had almost refused. The older woman had sensed her hesitation, but hadn't played on it. She had no one except herself and the quixotic impulse that had prompted her acceptance to blame for the fix she was in now. She stared at her reflection in the mirror, wondering if she had taken leave of her sanity. Even her clothes were especially chosen for the evening, casual without being too casual, and her favorite fragrance was in the right places. She could've been dressing for a date.

"I am just continuing what we started today," she assured herself as she turned away. She ignored the voice in her mind who named her liar.

"I'm sorry we had to eat out," Pippa murmured, smiling ruefully at Diana across the table.

"Although I must admit Jason chose this place well. A touch too much light, but the food was lovely." She raised her coffee cup to her lips, hiding a smile.

Jason felt like disowning his aunt. "Pippa, behave. You've been doing a wonderful Dolly Levi imitation since Diana joined us. It doesn't go with a southern accent and blood-thirsty mind."

Diana laughed, enjoying the byplay that had been going on all evening between the two strong-willed people. "Actually, I rather like her antics. And she is right about the lights."

"Antics. I don't do antics. That's juvenile."

"Don't you start," Jason muttered, feeling surrounded and harassed on all sides. Diana's scent was wrapped around him like a second skin. Of course, the inordinate room Pippa's costume—there was no other word for it—had taken in the plush booth had a lot to answer for. He knew damn well his aunt had worn the multi-layered skirt on purpose, so Diana would practically have to drape herself around him to have room to sit down.

"I didn't mean to burn dinner. I've apologized at least a hundred times." She fumbled around under the mass of folds and fabric for her purse. "I'm going to the ladies'," she announced, rising to her feet. "Don't get up, Diana. I need to be alone for a minute, thanks to my graceless nephew." She stalked off, leaving the pair staring after her with varying expressions.

"You hurt her feelings," Diana said, turning to Jason. The shrewd look on his face stopped her next words. Suddenly, she started rethinking the whole night.

"I think I will kill her," he stated quite calmly. "What do you want to make a bet, the brazen schemer is making a call for a taxi right now?"

"I would say she had one lined up before she left the house. She is kin to you, don't forget." Diana sat back against the cushions, not as angry as she probably should have been. She wondered vaguely if she would ever outsmart either of this pair. "How does it feel to be on the receiving end of a plan you knew nothing about?" she asked meditatively as she sipped her coffee.

Jason glared at her, having expected her anger. "Were you in on this?"

"No. Do I look a fool who would stick her head in a lion's mouth twice to have it bitten off at the neck? I came here for one reason. I want to smooth out the rough spots between us so we can work together. I don't want to keep watching my back. I had enough of that when my life was only skating." Diana's words held every ounce of determination and sincerity she could muster. She meant what she said as far as it went.

Jason studied her, forgetting his irritation with Pippa. "You mean it?"

Diana said nothing, although she fought a smile at his annoyed tone. Having the upper hand with Jason was rather addictive.

Deciding he would take the sane course and steer clear of an affair with Diana was one thing. Having her sit calmly by indicating the same choice was irritating. Was he that easy to forget or ignore? Angered when he should have been relieved, he gave into an impulsive need to puncture her cool poise. "I still want you."

Diana looked into Jason's eyes and admitted to herself that she was going to take a mad gamble. Playing it safe with the danger he represented was not enough. She had tried running and failed. It was time to face him and the future. She might not win, but she wouldn't lose by default. "Ditto."

"Ditto?" This time his voice held the beginnings of barely-restrained roar. "You don't look it."

A strange sense of freedom and relief drove the tension from her body. "Neither do you." Despite her best efforts, her lips twitched revealingly.

"Are you laughing at me?"

Her grin tickled her cheeks and flashed in her eyes. "Actually, I'm probably laughing at both of us."

"I don't like it."

"I can see that." She reached over to pat his arm, wondering where she was getting her nerve. The fire that leapt in the darkness of his eyes should have frightened her. "You have no sense of humor. But don't worry. You're intelligent. I'm sure you'll get the knack of it before too long."

"You're pushing it."

"Probably. But we both know we've been trained to push the limits."

Jason inhaled sharply and then mentally cursed the unwise action as Diana's scent filled his senses.

Her challenge was tearing up his control. This was a game he had not anticipated. If she led the way, there would be no way to temper the passion that lay between them. She was not a woman for half measures. "Not this way. Don't start something that might blow up in our faces. I am what I am."

Diana didn't pretend to misunderstand. "Anyone can change, if they want to badly enough."

"But will they be able to handle the changes or themselves, when they're done?"

For the first time, Diana saw uncertainty replace control and strength in his eyes. A woman's need to protect rose. She had not thought of what she was asking and the costs Jason would have to pay to give her the emotion she needed to survive. But equally, for her, there was no other way. She couldn't give herself to a man who didn't know the meaning of caring, loving, and just plain enjoyment. Her soul would starve and ultimately her body would rebel, and she would be left with nothing except the ashes of passion turning her world grey.

Jason shifted uncomfortably, resenting her solemn stare and yet knowing she had a right to the look in her eyes. He hadn't given her false promises.

"I think you don't know what you want any more than I do. Are you as tired of hiding in that frozen wasteland of solitude as I am of holding onto my past? You made me look at what the complex meant to me and to others. I saw what I had done to my life. Can't you do the same? Can you reach beyond yourself, into a future that might hurt you as much as you're afraid I'll get hurt? Can you offer me more than a hot affair with a friendly good-bye at the end?''

"How much more?" he interrupted to demand. The question erupted before he could stop it. But once said, he had no desire to call it back.

"A commitment."

"Marriage?"

"That was your choice, not mine."

"Either way, that's a high price on your coming to me."

The verbal knife slid into her heart before she could defend against the thrust. Diana inhaled deeply, fighting the pain. "And you put too low a price on it," she hit back, knowing any weakness would be taken as a sign of surrender.

Feeling cornered, Jason's hand clenched into a fist as his eyes glittered with swift rage. "I think it's time I took you home." He reached for his wallet and tossed some bills on the table.

Diana rose and collected her wrap and purse. He didn't touch her as they started for the door. Just as they reached the foyer, two men entered from the hall leading toward the restrooms.

Both were worse for wear; neither saw Jason, only Diana.

"Hello, pretty lady. Did you come to keep us company?" one asked, reaching for her arm as the other moved to circle her.

Diana froze, more out of surprise than fear.

"Unless you want a cast on both of your arms,

I'd tuck my hands in my pocket," Jason warned in a low growl that petrified both men. "You got the title right, but the moves wrong. You've got ten seconds to clear out or I start moving the garbage myself."

Neither needed a second warning. Diana watched them go, stunned at how truly lethal Jason had sounded. She turned, her breath hissing out in a soft gasp as she got a look at Jason's face. The bones stood out prominently beneath the rage-taut skin. His eyes could have doused the fires of hell. His hands were balled into fists at his side and every muscle in his body seemed poised to fight. He looked ready to kill to protect her. Awed, off balance at the emotions pouring through her, she tried to smooth her expression.

Jason glanced away from his prey as Diana gasped. "Don't worry, they're gone." He forced the tension away and fought for a soothing tone. "I wouldn't have let them hurt you no matter how much we argued."

Diana blinked, not even remembering the men. "You said something about taking me home," she murmured vaguely.

He took her hand. "I think I'd better. It's getting late and you'll want to change for the rink." This time, as he escorted her out, he stayed close. "I wonder if Pippa still means to watch you work?" He wasn't really interested, but anything was better than the silence he filled with thoughts of taking her in his arms to comfort her.

Diana got into the car, waiting until he came

around and slid into the driver's seat. "Is there any reason she shouldn't?"

He shrugged. "If it doesn't bother you, it won't bother me."

"Tell me what Jason said when I left you two alone," Pippa demanded, plunking herself down on the bench next to Diana. "Was he furious?"

"I'd say that is a fairly accurate assessment." Diana started taking off her street boots and strapping on her skates. "For a while, he thought I was in on the idea."

Pippa frowned. "He didn't tear a strip off, did he?"

Diana shook her head. "But it was a near miss. I don't think your rather heavy-handed attempt at pairing us up is a very good idea."

"You don't think so? I've always had success in the past," Pippa murmured, looking thoughtful.

She studied Pippa, beginning to wonder just how devious her new friend was. "I hope I don't find out there is a plot within a plot in this farce.

Pippa spread her hands, looking innocent. "Would I do that? Haven't I been honest with you after my little performance? I could have lied and you wouldn't have known it."

Diana had to admit that was true. Her doubts lingered, but she couldn't put her finger on why. Finally, she had to accept Jason had conditioned her to expect plots where there were none. "I guess I'm getting a little paranoid." She tried a slight smile in apology.

Pippa patted her hand. "Don't worry about it. Jason tends to bring that out in most of us." She leaned back, settling her fur hat more securely on her head. "Now, let's see some really beautiful skating. Jason says you're a dream on silver blades."

Diana's cheeks flushed at the unexpected compliment. "With a description like that, watch me fall on my face," she murmured, laughing softly when Pippa grinned. She rose and headed for the center of the rink.

Jason watched the two women from the shadows. He had been invited to come, by Pippa reluctantly and Diana politely. He had refused both, having no intention of getting any closer to Diana until he could come to grips with the latest development in their rather strange relationship. How he had ended up here just because he couldn't sleep and needed something to do, still escaped him. He followed the path Diana traced on the ice. Tonight, her music was moody rather than lyrical or passionate. This time, every emotion seemed to be flowing out of her in a river of feeling to score the ice. His body and mind absorbed the wealth of sound and sensory input. His heart sped up, his muscles tensed, his eyes darkened with memories of those moments when he had held her in his arms; and those moments in his sleep when he had awakened and found his dream was really a nightmare of loneliness. Sweat beaded on his forehead as the web of emotion drew tight around him. He could feel every lift and sway of her skating. He could feel the sting of the cold wind off the ice, feel the muscles straining for that perfect extension, that intensity of range, that beauty which lived in the mind, but rarely came through in the movement of the blades. His breathing deepened, taking on the cadence of exertion. Without realizing it, he moved closer, well within the range of Pippa's sight. Even as Pippa slipped out of the rink into the night, he was unsheathing his blades.

He raised his head, eyes locked on Diana as he straightened. And as she turned, flying down the ice toward him, he slid onto the frozen surface, his stride automatically matching hers. There were no hesitations this night. The music blended with their movements, the emotions he had always locked inside burst forth at the first touch of her hand. His fingers tightened on hers and she read the challenge in his eyes when he drew her close.

Diana felt his power mate with hers. She returned the strength with the tempering of her own force. Nothing was impossible. No lift too high, no leap too intricate. The tape slipped into the next arrangement, this one more demanding than anything that had gone before. His hand was there as she stepped into her liftoff. His strength threw her out and away, his gaze settled her gently iceward once more, her arms arched wide, human wings to attest to her flight. They came together, her body yielding to his as they moved into a spin. Another toss and another. She was flying, the sun was no more than the spotlights trained on the ice, but it didn't matter. Jason was always there, waiting for that moment of touchdown. The music crested. The emotions surged to meet it. The power threw them both into twin leaps of bold perfection. They came down together, eyes locked as the final move brought them into an embrace both dangerous and beautiful to watch. The music died.

"Damn you," Jason whispered hoarsely. "It would have been better if you had not let me share this with you."

"It is why you came," she breathed unevenly, knowing and understanding him as she never had before. "This is what you could have been."

"Yes."

"You knew."

"I knew."

"Why with me?"

"I don't know. I wish I did, for your sake."

The scent of male and energy expended was rich and compelling. Diana fought the combination of her senses and the emotions burying their slender claws so deep in her soul. His arms tightened as though he could sense her battle.

She gathered the last dregs of her strength and made one final plea for freedom she didn't really want. "I meant what I said."

"I know. But I need you. And this. There will be no other but you and you alone who can give me this? I know that if I know nothing else." He hesitated, wanting to snatch that which was so important to him, but knowing this time, if he closed his hand too soon, he would never get another chance to touch the limitless bounty of his inner self. "Let it be enough, Diana. Share with me and teach me to share with you."

NINE

Diana stared into his eyes, realizing the distance he had come in so short a time. A few days ago he had verbally forced a confession out of her. This time, there was only his husky plea and the seduction of his passion to lure her on. She wanted him. All the words and rationale in the world would not change that for her. He was offering her less than she had hoped for, but more than she thought him capable of giving. A terrible or perhaps glorious risk.

"Don't shut me out." The need to command her surrender was almost as strong as his need to have her give in because of her own desire.

"I can't. Hold me and keep on holding me." Her arms tightened around him, her eyes aglow with wanting him.

Jason rose, lifting her as he had once before. The look in his eyes was at once tender, possessive, and as old as creation. This one woman, out of all the others, held his future in her hands. He didn't understand it, didn't dare look too deeply, but he did know her power. "Where? I won't take you here as though you don't matter."

She smiled, touching his cheek with trembling fingers. "It's too cold, anyway."

"Honey, we would melt the ice." He glided to the rail. Diana reached down to open the gate to the outer floor. He walked through and sat down on a bench still holding her close.

"I think we've been through this before."

Jason cupped her face in his palms, his thumbs brushing over her lips. "Never. What was before was rushed and my own stupidity." He dipped his head, his tongue tracing the sweep his thumbs had just made. "I want you more than I can tell you. I've never regretted my lack of sentimentality until now. I want to give you beautiful words."

"I would rather have the beauty you bring to me instead," she whispered just before his lips closed over hers. Diana opened her mouth to him, unafraid that his passion for it matched her own. His tongue was hard, a delicate spear to pierce the warmth that flooded her with every stroke of his hands on her body. Her breasts firmed, ripened as she arched against him. His breath was invisible heat on her skin to dispel the cold of the frozen environment. When his fingers circled her nipples, nipping gently at the erect peaks, she cried out softly.

Jason raised his head, his lashes shielding his eyes from the suddenly too-bright lights. "Where?" he demanded hoarsely.

"My place, yours. I don't care."

He'd never felt less like thinking. "Pippa's at my place."

"Then mine." Diana wound her arms around his neck, pulling his mouth down to hers. "I don't care, but make it soon before I embarrass both of us."

Stunned at the male pleasure surging through him at her honesty, he hugged her tight against him. "Sweetheart, you couldn't embarrass me if you stripped naked right here. You make me feel a hundred feet tall and more man than I can tell you." His hands slid down her legs, kneading the firm muscles on his way to unfasten her skates. "You're pure woman. Fire, passion, demands, and softness. I think I would kill for you if the need ever arose." One skate thudded to the floor, followed quickly by the other. His own were equally and speedily dealt with. When he had them off, he rose and set her on her feet in front of him. "One car or two?"

Diana held out her hands, the fingers trembling with need aflame but denied. "If you're depending on me arriving alive, you'd better drive," she admitted huskily.

He threaded her fingers with his and took them to his lips. "Where did you learn to be so honest?"

Diana wanted to tell him then, to confess she hoped and prayed by giving everything in her to give that he would open to her, would trust her. "It's the way I am. I've never lied to you about that."

Jason slipped his arm around her waist, not prepared to tolerate any more separation than absolutely necessary. Words tumbled in his head—new words, passionate words, tender words, beautiful words, words he had spoken to no other woman because they had never been in his mind. When he wanted to speak, to return her gift, he found he couldn't. He looked at her as she stood facing him in the moonlit darkness of the car. The silver light was soft and gentle on her skin, making her appear even more fragile and feminine.

Diana read the regret, the frustration in his eyes as he caressed her lips with quivering fingers and then moved on to trace the bones of her cheeks, her brows, and the tiny hollows behind her ears. She trembled with each new touch, the need growing stronger, the passion burning brighter and more demanding.

"I would dress you in diamonds, emeralds, and furs if you would let me." He couldn't give her feelings out loud, but he could give her something.

"I don't want them."

His lips twisted into a sad smile. "I know. It was a foolish thing to say." He drew back his hand, inhaling sharply when Diana caught it and carried it to her breast. Even through the thickness of her coat, he could feel the tiny nub demanding his attention.

"You can give me this. I know what you are. I don't want anything more than you can give me."

"It's less than what you asked for," Jason reminded her, disturbed at her change of heart. He should have been delighted he had won, but the victory had a bittersweet taste. It clung, teasing his senses with promises of what might have been.

"Why are you worried now? It is what you said you wanted." She held her breath, recognizing the fight being waged so silently within him. Did he realize what was happening? Did he understand that when they came together that neither of them would ever be the same again?

Jason frowned, damning himself for a fool. What was he trying to do? Make Diana change her mind? Was he crazy? His body was aching with need. He was becoming more aroused just looking at her, and he was sitting in a cold car in the middle of a deserted parking lot. He had rocks in his head.

"You're right," he murmured, turning to start the car.

Diana exhaled softly, fighting the disappointment flooding her. Just for a moment, there had been a crack in the wall. The emotions pouring out of him on the ice had been no fluke. Jason was capable of a tremendous depth of feeling. She had tapped it once. She would again. And again. Until there would be no more barriers to hide behind or until she burned herself out in trying to reach him.

Diana entered her home first, her ears attuned to Jason's near-silent tread behind her. He had not touched her once on the drive here. He had not spoken. She had sat in the darkness, watching the scenery while she grew as cold as the landscape.

She didn't want to lose the fire, but she didn't know how to rekindle the blaze.

She turned to find him staring at her across the width of the living room. "What now?" she asked carefully.

He walked toward her, off balance, frustrated by his own withdrawal and her reaction. He lifted his hand to touch her, paused when she studied the action as though unaffected. "Have you changed your mind?"

"I think that should be my question."

This time his fingers made contact, wrapping around her arm and drawing her close. "Never in a thousand years. But I will walk away, if that's what you want." Her eyes were cloudy with emotion he could almost feel. Her body slowly softened against his. His muscles unclenched, making him aware of how tensely he had been awaiting her answer.

"You frightened me."

He took her mouth softly, tenderly, wanting to soothe them both. "I frightened myself."

Diana accepted the kiss, letting it seep into her being. When he lifted her into his arms, it was natural to curl her arm around his neck and lay her head on his shoulder. Murmuring directions in his ear, she closed her eyes and opened her senses to the joy of having him with her. She had almost lost him. Had she given the wrong answer or shown the least hesitation, she knew he would have left her.

Her bedroom was in semidarkness as they entered, lit only by the over spill of the light from the living room. The shadows were gentle, secretive, but kindly so. The room was warm, silent except for the mingled sound of their breathing. Jason stopped beside the bed and slowly lowered Diana to her feet. His eyes locked with hers as he unbuttoned her coat and drew it off. She said nothing, only watched him with solemn eyes as one by one each piece of clothing was removed and tossed aside. Her flesh was cream velvet surrounded by ebony satin night. His hands caressed her breasts, circling the soft mounds, cherishing the taut peaks. Her lips parted, her breath coming in tiny pants of rising desire.

His body tightened in response, but he ignored it. He wanted to give her something of value in return for the emotion she had laid at his feet. His gifts would be pleasure so great tears would stand in her eyes before the night kissed the morning hello, desire as deep as her heart was generous, and loving so special that no one would ever touch her so completely again.

"You're still dressed," Diana breathed huskily, her hands burying themselves in the thickness of his coat. She tugged at the buttons, finally freeing them. Then, she inhaled sharply as Jason's hand slid down her stomach, to press against her womb, kneading in a circular motion that set her aflame. Her legs went weak as she sagged against him. He caught her close, the fur of his coat stroking her suddenly sensitive skin so she felt as though his hands were everywhere. She hardly noticed the feel of the bed beneath her back. Her eyes locked with his, she gave herself up to the tension building within her.

When his lips touched her breasts for the first time, she cried out, arching to meet his mouth as though she would die to feel his kiss. Her eyes were closed in delight, her head thrown back against the pillows. Diana was so caught up in the waves of pleasure washing over her she was unaware of his clothes being dragged from his body until he was as bare as she.

Jason watched her face, finding more pleasure in her changing expressions than he had ever found in the most practiced of his previous bedmates. "Tell me what you like," he commanded, corralling his own needs to satisfy hers.

Diana forced open her eyes, stunned at his words. "I like it all. Every touch . . ." She gasped as his hand slid lower, teasing the inner core of her heat. ". . . is magic," she finished brokenly just before her world splintered into fragments of light and sensation. Tears rained down her face at the pleasure.

When he joined them as one, she held him tight, feeling the tension return only harder and more demanding than before. He thrust deep, each stroke agonizingly slow. Her body arched, twisting in a silent demand for more and more yet again. He denied her while wrapping her tighter in the world of her own passion. Her breaths were gasps, small moans and cries of ecstasy. And still, he kept the pace slow, letting each plane happen but controlling the degree so both of them hovered just on the edge of madness. Her skin glowed, the dew of energy expended bringing a sheen to their joined flesh. The scent of loving filled the air—rich, musky, beguiling. Diana slipped loose her last inhibitions, meeting his strokes with tiny convulsive clinches deep in her body.

Jason groaned against her ear, his body arching helplessly against hers. "Not now, honey," he pleaded, trying to still her by gripping her hips in his hands.

"Yes, now," she commanded, grasping him intimately again, even as she buried her hands in his hair and brought his mouth to hers. Her tongue thrust deep as she gathered her last bit of strength and arched hard against him.

Jason exploded, her moves too strong to be denied. The conqueror became the conquered. Softness and feminine power once more reigned supreme. And yet, that supremacy had been born in Jason's arms and out of his strength. Diana followed Jason blindly through the passionate corridors, falling through time and space until her senses returned to normal and she found herself wrapped in Jason's arms, her head pillowed on his shoulder while his hand stroked her hair.

"Diana," he whispered, damning his loss of control. At the last, he had not ever known such a driving need to bury himself so deeply within her that they would never be separated. He could have hurt her. She had been so limp when he had rolled onto his back, carrying her with him. They were still joined as one but she had not moved.

"Diana, are you all right?" he demanded, worried, for the second time in his life, frightened.

Diana rubbed her cheek over his chest, inhaling his scent as though she would imprint it forever in her memory. "Hmm . . ."

"Talk to me."

"Too much energy."

"Did I hurt you?"

She heard the urgency in his voice and tried to rouse enough to respond to it. "Hurt me? You loved me. It was beautiful."

He sighed deeply, relaxing. "Woman, you are something."

"I pleased you?" Diana lifted her head to gaze into his eyes. She smiled at the stunned look on his face.

"Pleased. I'm so pleased, it may take me a week to get the energy to get out of your bed." He slipped his hand over her bottom, lightly outlining the lush curve.

"You mean, that's all I get?" she teased, discovering her strength returning. She couldn't remember a time when she had felt so alive, so fulfilled, so content with her world.

"Wanton."

"Voluptuary. I always liked that word. Never felt that way, but I sure liked the word."

"Fishing for compliments?" The words popped out, surprising her as much as him at their bantering quality.

"I'm going to resist temptation and not point out . . ."

His fingers covered her mouth before she could get the risqué play on words said. "Now, remember, you wouldn't want to sully my ears with that kind of talk.'

Diana laughed softly, delighted with his teasing. She had not thought him capable of playful behavior.

Jason froze as the sound of her laughter wrapped around him. Once, when he had been no more than seven, on his way to practice, he had stopped at a playground, drawn by the giggles and shouts of children he had known but had not had time to join in their games. He could remember standing there, his skates in his hand, his eyes trained on two girls, one with shiny blond hair and the other dark. They had been so happy, teasing each other, smiling, the sun flashing off gap-toothed smiles. He had felt lonely then—scarcely old enough to read and a son of a large family—but he had known what loneliness and always being on the outside of life meant. He had been late to practice that day and had been assigned extra training as punishment. He had hardly noticed because the faces of those two girls and their fun, fun he couldn't share, had been more a burden than anything his coach could have handed out.

Diana touched Jason's face, caught by the bleakness in his eyes. For one moment, he had been young, carefree, a man enjoying himself without a thought for tomorrow. "What is it?" she whispered, wanting to drag him away from whatever hurt him so and call back the sun and the warmth that had been theirs.

Jason blinked, focusing on her face. He tried a smile, wanting to reassure her and forestall any questions. "Nothing. A memory. No more."

"You could share it," she suggested.

"No." He pressed her hand to his cheek, inhaling her fragrance and savoring the intimacy of her flesh joined with his. "An old story for people like us. Practice was our life. The cost was high. Sometimes I wonder what I missed."

"A lot," she said, her memories no kinder than his. "But you gained so much. Surely, that compensated?"

"I thought it did. Now, I'm not so sure. I look around and see other men my age with homes and families. I wake up alone and I often sleep alone because I want more than just a lovely woman whose name I barely remember in my bed. And yet, what would I have to give to a woman and a deep relationship? I have traveled the world and could tell you the interior of every ice skating rink or sports hall in every major city. I can quote the emergency instructions for airliners in almost any language you could name, although I only speak English and French. What I can't do is tell you what the people can buy in their marketplaces, what the land looks like, and how the natives think or feel. I made a small fortune because of my ability to be a 'brilliant technician,' but what do I know of people?"

Diana listened carefully. She had thought Jason

secure in his barren world where strategy and chess moves on the human board of life were the only ways of existence he wanted. She had not known Jason could feel the same loss of self she had struggled to define at eighteen. When she had bowed out of the limelight, no one but her parents, Nicky, and Maggie had understood. "You're learning now," she murmured, knowing that useless sympathy would not answer.

"Am I? I look in your eyes and I see more passion than I have ever known. You make me feel things that scare the hell out of me. I can't cope, but I also can't back away. And I want to almost as much as I want to get as close as I can to you, to share that glorious kaleidoscope of feeling that wraps around you like a cloak." He carried her hand to his mouth, his tongue tracing a delicate pattern in her palm. He watched her eyes cloud with desire and felt the answering surge of his own need. "It's so simple with you. How can it be like this between us? Just us. I'm the North Pole and you're the tropics. It can't work."

"So negative, my lover. I would not have thought a man with your kind of determination could be stopped with anything short of death, if you wanted something badly enough." She cupped his cheek with her free hand. Her fingers outlined the strong bones that gave his features character and definition.

"I don't know what I want," he exploded harshly, his breath searing her skin before he pulled her palm away from his lips. His grasp tightened. "I should be thinking of the complex, almost day and night. That's the way I've always been, a tunnel visionary. Nothing should get in the way. Nothing should matter.''

''But it does,'' she stated softly, smiling gently.

''Yes,'' he admitted on a deep sigh. His temper was spent and he was confused at both its appearance and retreat. His control seemed to have more holes in it than Swiss cheese.

''Is it so very terrible, having more than one interest? It is the way most of the world works.''

''It isn't the way I work.''

Diana tried to control a laugh, only partially succeeding. ''You could change your ways. You aren't all that old.'' Despite her light words, she was more hopeful than ever. Jason was showing more range of emotion now, in these last few minutes, than he had since she had known him. Passion between them was exquisite but unless there was more, one day the desire would burn itself out. And then, she would be alone again. Only this time there would be memories she suspected no man would ever exorcise. Jason was all wrong for her. He was hard. She was soft. He buried himself. She threw her heart and soul into life. He didn't believe in commitments and she felt only half alive without them. And yet, she loved him. She didn't need any great revelation. She certainly prayed he didn't realize her love, but she did love him. Her love wasn't rational. It wasn't sane and it damn well wasn't wise.

''Into what? I don't know what I want to do with my life beyond the complex.'' He had told no one except her of his frustration. "I've spent every waking moment knowing exactly where to place each foot toward the goal I had set myself. Now, I find I don't know what I want, what I need, or what I am." He glared at her his eyes raking her from head to toe, his gaze lingering for just a fraction of a second on her bare breast. "You want to know something? This is the first time in my life I have had anything as delectable as you in my bed and spent valuable moments discussing my future." He reached for her, half expecting a denial. "I can think of better things to do with our time."

Diana started to protest his sudden about-face, then changed her mind. Jason had given her more than a peek into his mind, a look he had given no one else. It had to be hard, being that honest when he clearly distrusted most people. The fact that he had made the attempt with her had to be respected. For now, it was time to return to the world in which they could come together without questions, the world of pleasure and passion.

"No questions? No protests?"

"I want you, too. You're right. We've talked long enough."

TEN

Diana walked down the hall toward Nicky's old office. Even before she reached the door, she could hear Jason arguing with someone on the phone. She stopped, not wanting to interrupt, despite the fact that she was slightly late for their lunch date. An oath filled the silence and she covered her mouth to control her amusement. Over the past six weeks, Jason had shed his frozen facade as though it had never been. Lately, he had a temper he wasn't shy about using. He also laughed more, muttered a lot, especially over the various construction delays on the complex, and made love to her with a fiery passion that did not abate. They skated together regularly now, at night, when the rink was empty.

So much had changed for her, too. She spent more time with Jason than she had thought she could blend into her already packed schedule. Her work had never been better and her sleep never more satisfying. She and Jason still kept their same addresses but more often than not, they spent the night together. Pippa had disappeared as swiftly as she had come, whispering in Diana's ear a promise to return immediately if Diana had any more trouble with Jason.

"What the devil are you doing out here in the hall? Why didn't you come into my office?" Jason demanded as he lifted Diana into his arms and kissed her hard. "Did I need that. My publicist is driving me nuts. I told him about your benefit skating exhibition idea and he jumped on it. He's been on the phone for the last two days, lining up talent," he continued after he set Diana back on her feet.

Diana laughed and tucked her hand in the crook of his arm. Now that she had thrown off the mantle of her past determination not to get involved with the training end of amateur skating, she found herself thinking of ways to help Jason realize his plans; and at the same time benefit the boys and girls climbing up the ladder to reach for the Olympic dream.

"I'm glad he approves. But I could really get addicted to your brand of greeting. Although I suppose I ought to object to being picked up like a doll every time you're in the mood."

He grinned down at her. "You know you love it, short stuff. Besides, I'm not the one who is tiny enough to fit in my pocket. And if the truth is known, I like picking you up. Call it my macho coming out."

Diana almost choked at the verbal image. "I

think I liked you better all stone-faced and frozen," she murmured. "Macho, indeed. I have never known a more person-conscious man in my life. You have more faith in me than I have in myself."

Jason shrugged, not particularly impressed with the accolade. "You've met Pippa. If that woman has ever been stopped from doing anything she wanted to do, I don't remember the time. Lorelei is as strong-willed. With these two in my history, I've come to believe women can do anything they want."

Diana leaned against his side, marveling once again at Jason's honesty. In another man, she might have questioned his sincerity. "You don't look very downtrodden to me."

He grinned at her. "I hide it well." They left the rink by the side door. Jason's car was parked close to the building. "I hope the food is good in this place you heard about. I'm starved." He started the car, finding pleasure in her scent and the feel of her next to him. Since Diana had entered his life, he no longer felt smothered in a cloud of loneliness. He had someone to laugh with, to share with, and to love with. When he was tired, Diana cared. When he got frustrated, she listened to him blow off steam and didn't think any less of him for his loss of temper. When he needed silence, she simply shared time with him. He glanced at her out of the corner of his eye. Even now, she was completely relaxed, seemingly content to be with him.

"What are you thinking about?" he asked quietly, wondering what went on in her mind during these silent moments.

Diana turned her head, seeing that curious look that seemed to be growing daily in Jason's eyes. He was curious about her, often probing into her thoughts, her feelings past, present, and even future. "About the changes that you have brought to my life," she murmured honestly.

"That should be my line."

"Perhaps." She smiled slightly. "Until you forced me to see what a coward about amateur skating I had become, I had let those last years before I quit blight my life. Because of you, I'm finally making peace with that time."

He frowned, remembering the tale she had told him, a story of being driven into the ground with one man's determination to bask in her reflected glory. "Unfortunately, there are a few of those kind of people around, but they are few and far between and don't seem to last all that long. Word gets out when a coach is almost inhuman in his training methods, or anything else that is that far off the wall." He paused, a niggling question still bothering him.

"There is one thing I still don't understand. Why didn't you just get another coach, instead of quitting completely?"

"I thought about it, but there were other factors involved by that time." One being she had been too ill to make the attempt. "I finally decided the joy was no longer in skating for me. I didn't want to compete any more."

Every word she spoke was the truth, with only one piece left out. She had given her word that day the Olympic official made his request for her silence, protecting in the only way she had her sport and the youngsters who had come after and would continue to join the teams. Jason had shown her so much of himself that she wanted to trust him with what was left of her secret, but she could not go back on that promise.

"You could have taken time off. Maybe even sought the help of a sports psychologist."

"I could have," she agreed slowly. "But I didn't." It was time to finish with the subject.

Jason glanced at her, reading her need to shut the door on the past. He frowned slightly, still plagued by the feeling that there was something more back there. "Would you skate before an audience now?"

Diana considered the idea, even though her first reaction was a vehement no. For years, she had shunned public exhibitions of any sort. Was it possible she would glide into the rink now and enjoy it as she had so long ago? "The thought isn't as abhorrent as it once was, but I must admit I won't willingly go back in front of an audience. I don't know if I can explain how hard those two years with that man were. He made me doubt my skating, my talent, my skill, and myself. Nothing was ever good enough. Day after day he drummed that into me until one day I just couldn't take it any more. I froze on the ice. I stared into the eyes of a few of my family and friends and started to sweat and shake until I could barely stand. The music began and I couldn't remember the first move. My father had to help me out of the rink. It took a long time for me to get to a point where I could skate just for my own pleasure.'' She shuddered, the memories too vivid to be ignored. She fought back the past and tried to smile for Jason. ''I truly like what I do. It gives me the freedom to express my talent in a way that keeps me out of the limelight.''

Jason's frown deepened. He had thought he understood the toll she had paid. He had been wrong—the price was far higher than he had known.

''Why did you ask?'' she questioned on seeing his expression.

''No reason.''

Diana wasn't put off by the indifferent tone. She had come to know Jason and his moods well. ''Tell me.''

''You won't like it,'' he warned as he drove the car into an empty slot. He had been crazy to even consider asking her to participate in the show.

''You can't be sure.''

''I was going to ask you to skate in the benefit.'' He glanced at her, watching her eyes widen in surprise, then go blank with shock.

Diana searched his face, stunned at the suggestion that even a child should have seen coming. ''I'd say no,'' Diana said carefully. ''Today isn't the first time we've discussed my retirement. After what I told you, you had to know I wouldn't consider the idea. Was this another of your tricks?''

He shook his head, pain knifing through him that she could believe him capable of maneuvering her now after what they had shared. ''I suppose I deserved that. But I had hoped you would forgive me now that we have become . . .'' He hesitated, searching for the right word. ''Close.''

Diana wanted to believe him and looking into his eyes, seeing the pain he made no attempt to hide, convinced her as no argument could have. ''I'm sorry.''

He caught her hand, holding it tight. ''You have no reason to be. We both know I would have done my best to manipulate you in the beginning. But I will never try again. Not with you.''

Diana returned the pressure of his hand, letting the words sink into her heart. Jason was changing before her eyes. He was nothing like the man who had come looking for her all those weeks ago. ''I believe you,'' she whispered.

His smile broke through the harshness of emotions held on a tight rein. ''Thank you. You won't regret trusting me,'' he breathed as he lowered his head to take her lips in a fiercely tender kiss.

Diana forgot that they were in full view of anyone who cared to look and gave herself up to the passion he could call up at will. His promise was one more hope for the future. She held on for all she was worth.

*   *   *

Jason yanked the phone away from his ear and stared at it. The sound of his publicist's voice was audible despite the distance between them.

"I said I checked into your girlfriend's background. Quite by accident, as it happens."

Jason returned the phone to its former position, not wanting to miss Frank's defense. The man was a whiz at his job, but he had the nose of a ferret and the instincts of a mongoose when it came to getting every drop of publicity blood out of any event.

"I found out the lady is quite famous for more than her routines. There was a bit of a cloudburst over her retirement. As I'm sure you know." He hesitated, obviously waiting for Jason to explain why he had kept the tidbit from him.

Jason stayed silent, knowing Frank well enough to outsmart him.

Frank sighed irritably. "I should have known you wouldn't take the bait," he complained.

"You should have," Jason agreed.

"Why don't you sign her up for this little charity thing? Her name on the card will draw not only the local crowd, but a mess of press as well. No one has ever believed her story of just wanting to find out how the real world operates. I mean, the woman had audiences waiting to toss her bouquets of orchids and she walked off without even trying. There has to be a story there. You know the routine. Make it work for you, Jay."

Jason listened, strangely numb to the words. How many times in his life had he used an item to garner the kind of image he needed? Telling himself that most things were fair in business had worked in the past. This time, no amount of rationalizing mattered. All he knew was a feeling of deep disgust. He couldn't use Diana or something that clearly still caused her pain in order to further his own dream.

"No."

"What do you mean, no? Are you crazy?" With every question, Frank's voice sharpened and rose until he was all but shouting. "These charity events are a dime a dozen now. You need something to catch the public's eye. Here you are sitting on a gold mine and you won't use it. What's wrong with you lately? Didn't I stick with you when you bailed out of the ice show? You had eight or nine years left of good skating. We could have cleaned up and you wanted out. I helped you. I fended off the reporters and covered your tracks while you did that little civilian-type schooling or whatever it was. Is this how you repay me? I don't work for nothing, you know. I agreed to help you get this complex thing off the ground, but I didn't agree to sit on my thumbs and not even get peanuts for my trouble." He paused, took a deep breath, and continued. "Is it the woman? Hell, I'll ask her if you've got something going in that department and don't want to mess it up."

Jason leaned back in his chair and let the tirade wash over him. Everything his agent said was true. Vague feelings of guilt caught him off guard. Then, the last part of Frank's statement made itself felt. Jason stiffened in his chair, every muscle tense. His eyes narrowed as his temper built. "Hold it right there. You don't know anything about my private life, so back off. We don't need Diana Diamond. Look at the names you already have committed. Half the pro-circuit is willing to come. Be satisfied with that."

"Like hell. I need something sensational."

"Then find it somewhere else," Jason said bluntly, his tone warning no argument would win. He waited, knowing Frank wouldn't want to give up but knowing, too, that he would in the end.

"All right," the agent conceded angrily. "You're a fool, Starke. I thought I had taught you better than this, but it seems as if I was wrong." Without another word, he slammed down the phone.

Jason replaced his receiver more gently, his expression disturbed. Nothing in his life seemed clear any longer. His course was marked with pitfalls and problems when there should have been none. Why had he protected Diana? It wasn't as if he didn't need her help. In that, Frank had been right. Frowning, he got to his feet to pace the floor. With every step his self-disgust grew. She had signed a contract with a clause in it that allowed him to use her or her name at just compensatory rate for publicity for the center. Unless she wanted to spend a lot of money, she was committed to him and the complex. He could afford to push her on appearing. He glanced at the phone and then away, unable to forget the look on her face when he had asked about her public performances. He couldn't do it to her.

"Damn!" The single word held all the frustration he felt. He was stuck with this stupid white-knight role and he didn't even know why. Having her in bed didn't seem like enough of a reason. Liking her was evident, but that seemed too tame as well. He shrugged irritably, the emotions he had searched for and found now more a burden than the gift he had thought them to be. *Never wish for something, you just might get it* came to mind. He had gotten his wish all right. It was too bad he hadn't gotten the ability to handle his feelings at the same time. Confusion was not his best mood. And frustration only brought out a driving need to fight back. Only this time, there was nothing to fight except his own emotional shadow. It was winning. He wasn't.

Diana stared at the list of moves on the paper in front of her and frowned. Nothing about the routine she was designing appealed to her. Muttering, she crumbled the sheet and threw it over her shoulder, not glancing at the the half-full wastebasket she missed.

Why couldn't she forget Jason's words? She knew how important his plans were to him. Naturally, he was interested in any angle that would get him a larger audience for the benefit. But why her? Why couldn't she live down that one moment in her life when she had finally had the courage to say no more? What was so terrible about not being able to step in front of an audience any more without feeling as though her skin was being flayed from her body? Didn't she have a right to live her own life? She hadn't given up skating. She hadn't taken to hiding in the closet. She hadn't become a neurotic. She had simply found a place where she could use her talent without tearing up her emotions in order to do it.

She got up and went to the window, staring out at the white landscape as she tried to sort out her thoughts. The guilt she felt was surprising and unwelcome. As was the niggling sense that something was not right. Jason hadn't said he didn't understand the position she had taken then and now, but the implication was clear in his eyes when he looked at her.

The thought angered her. What did he know? He was staring love in the face and he was as unaware of it as a blind man to a candle in the darkness. The phone rang, putting an end to her introspection. She went to the desk, propping her hip on the edge as she identified herself.

"Ms. Diana Diamond. I'm Frank Nelson. Jason's publicist. You may have heard him speak of me."

Curious as to why he would be calling her, Diana responded, "I know you're doing the promo on the complex and the benefit." Perhaps one of her clients appearing in the show wanted to use her name because she was on staff.

"I'm glad he's told you that much. The thing is that Jay and I got to talking and naturally your name came up. I must say I was impressed. Not only because of your current status in the skating community, but also for your participation earlier in your career.''

Diana stiffened, both at the mention of her past and Jason's connection with its coming up. "Meaning?" Jason wouldn't set her up like this. She had to remember his promise.

Frank laughed lightly, playing for time. "Now, don't be modest, Ms. Diamond. I'm a believer in plain speaking. You, Jason, and people like you have a right to admit your accomplishments. You've worked hard to get where you are.''

"I wish you would get to the point," she said bluntly, fighting the doubts beginning to seep into her mind.

Frank dropped all attempts at humor. "All right. I have a check on my desk made out in your name. There is a comma followed by three zeroes. Two spaces in front of the comma are blank. Pick your favorite number and it's yours for one performance by you. You select the music and we'll foot the bill for anything you'll need to get you on the ice.''

"You're crazy." Diana sat down in the chair as though she were nothing but a limp body. "Does Jason know about this?"

"He knows I wanted to talk to you. And he certainly knows about the contract containing the clause giving him the right to use you. It's standard, of course, as I'm sure your lawyer must have told you.''

Any hope Diana had left shattered as she remembered the paragraph she and her lawyer had discussed. When she had broached the matter with Jason, he had assured her that, other than publicizing her current profession, he had no other plans for a different kind of promotion. But Jason had lied. This afternoon and now. Betrayal was an acid taste in her mouth. She wanted to hang up the phone, but made herself listen instead.

"And just who is signing this check?"

"I'm not at liberty to say."

"Then, I'm not at liberty to accept," Diana came back quickly before giving in to the urge to sever the connection. Tears started in her eyes before she could drop the phone in the cradle. Wrapping her arms around herself, Diana rocked in the chair, feeling as though her body and mind were being torn in half. She had trusted Jason, telling him things about herself that she had told no one. He had betrayed her, using the one thing that was guaranteed to hurt her most.

"Fool!" she cried through her tears. "Idealistic fool."

She had been so sure he was coming to care for her. He had lied. Perhaps the emotions he had shown her were nothing more than illusions she had created in her own mind, or worse yet, tricks by the gamemaster. Winning at all costs. The phone rang. Thinking it was the agent again, Diana snatched the receiver up and said, "I don't care how many numbers or zeroes you put on that check, I don't want it."

"Diana, what's wrong?" Jason demanded, hearing the quiver in her voice and what sounded suspiciously like crying. Her words made no sense.

All her feelings came pouring out in a hot spate of words. "What do you care? You rat. I trusted you and you sicced that slimy little toad you call an agent on me."

Numbers? Zeroes? What had Frank done? "I did not sic Frank on you," Jason protested, too surprised at the accusation to be more articulate.

His mind raced. How had Diana talked to Frank? Fear shot through him, angering him even as he fought the feeling. Frank's words, the promise he had thought he had extracted from the agent and the empty pledge he had really gotten instead, blazed through his thoughts. He had been set up. Rage blotted out anger. Diana's pain was a live thing. He had to deal with that before he could go after the culprit.

Diana ignored the interruption, hurting too much to be generous or reasonable. "I told you how I felt about performing and you still let him hound me. You can take that check and throw it in the river for all I care." Crying harder than ever, Diana hung up once more. Allowing herself one more minute of grief, she laid her head on the desk and ignored the phone shrieking next to her ear. The ringing stopped. The silence was more deafening than the sound had been. Diana raised her head, listening. Suddenly, she was assailed by an almost uncontrollable urge to flee.

Jason. He was coming. She knew it as surely as

she knew the sun would set soon. Jason believed in winning. He wouldn't accept defeat gracefully or well. And because she loved him even now, and believed in his plans for the complex, she was vulnerable. She had to hide. Without thinking any farther than that, she pushed to her feet and hurried to the closet for her coat. Fortunately, her car had plenty of gas and she had an escape route that few people knew about. She would be safe there, safe to think and hopefully to heal a little before she had to confront him.

Jason slammed the door to his condo and threw his coat across the room. Three lousy hours of searching and he hadn't been able to find Diana. He hadn't realized how little he knew of her life before him, until he had tried to find her. Other than Nicky and his wife, he knew no one that she knew. Both had denied knowledge of her whereabouts, so he had been reduced to driving around town, looking for a human needle in a very populous urban haystack. He hadn't found her and that had angered him more. Nor had he been able to connect with Frank. According to his secretary, the agent was out of his office without any ETA for return.

Frowning deeply, Jason slumped into the chair nearest the fireplace and tried to think. Considering how they had met and how he had schemed to get Diana involved in his complex, Diana had every reason to distrust him. But he had truly thought she was coming to know him enough to realize he would keep his word. But more importantly, he had hoped she would realize he cared too much for her to ever use her as he had intended to in the beginning. So, what had gone wrong? He was new at this feeling mess but surely she, being the emotional person she was, had been able to read the signs.

"Why didn't she give me a chance to explain?" A simple question with an answer that eluded him no matter how many times he asked it.

ELEVEN

Diana walked the snowy trail as she had everyday for the past four. She was no closer to an answer about her future than she had been in the beginning. Her nights were filled with loneliness and memories. Her days were a kaleidoscope of doubts, fears, and temper. Betrayal rode side by side with love. Her past fought with her future and neither won. Logic didn't work and neither did emotion. It was as though she was caught in some strange time warp that had no beginning or end. She seemed to be waiting, but for what?

Jason knocked once on Nicky's door. He barely glanced at the new office as he responded to the call to enter. He had more important things on his mind than whether the interior decorator he had hired to redo the inside of the building had done his job.

"Where is she?"

Nicky rose to his feet behind the desk, eyeing Jason warily. "Where's who?"

Jason did his best to hold his anger. "You know who. Diana."

"How would I know?"

"You know. You and Maggie are her best friends. She wouldn't go off without telling someone. She isn't that kind of woman."

Nicky watched Jason as he circled the desk. He focused on the hands clenched at the younger man's sides. "I don't want to fight with you, but I will if I have to. You're right, Maggie and I do know where she is. But she doesn't want *you* to know."

Jason inclined his head, relaxing slightly. "I take it she confided in you." It was a statement, not a question.

Nicky nodded.

"You said nothing."

"Not my business."

"If the positions had been reversed, it would have been mine."

"Why?"

Jason hesitated, oddly unsure. Then he shook his head. He had had enough introspection to last him a lifetime. Four days of soul-searching had done nothing but give him a headache, sleepless nights, and a foul disposition. "Friends protect each other."

"Is that what you call what's between you and Diana?" Nicky sat down once again, but remained alert.

He shifted his shoulders, annoyed at the probing look he was having to endure when he would have much rather taken a punch at Nicky's very formidable jaw. "What's between us is just that, between us."

"That's a rather odd statement, considering that you seem to have lost her."

Jason took a chair, sighing wearily as he raked his fingers through his hair. His temper was doing him no good. He needed help. "I didn't do it. I did not tell Frank to approach Diana about the show."

Nicky relaxed at the flat tone. The storm that had been brewing had blown itself out. "I didn't think you did. But I don't think it matters now. Look at this." He tossed a large mailing envelope across the desk.

Warned by the ominous tone in Nicky's voice, Jason pulled out a folded sheet. His eyes narrowed to slits as he stared at the poster. A recent picture of Diana was displayed prominently and her name on the roster of stars slated to appear at the Starke Skating Complex benefit was second to Jason's.

"Where did you get this?" Only one man could have sent it, but how did Frank get it printed so quickly?

"Overnight mail. It arrived this morning. Read the letter that's with it."

Jason started swearing before he had finished the first three sentences. "I'll take him apart limb from limb. No wonder he's stayed out of sight. He hasn't missed a single media contact in the country."

"Another little something you didn't know."

Nicky folded his hands, staring at them for a second before lifting his eyes to Jason's furious face. "What are you going to do about it? The benefit is a little more than four weeks away. There is no way, with this kind of buildup, that you can afford to let Diana refuse to skate. And it isn't just for your sake now. It's for hers as well. I was here through that first mess. The press hounded her like dogs after a rabbit. She had to go into hiding and she was very ill at the time. She almost died."

Jason froze, not having heard that part before. He had known there had been more to Diana's story than she had told him. "What do you mean, she was ill?"

Nicky looked surprised, then angry. "I thought she had told you all about her so-called retirement. Knowing Diana, I should have known better. That crazy fool."

"I thought she had, too," he retorted grimly. "I must admit her reaction, given the woman I know, seemed very extreme."

"Believe me, it wasn't." Nicky's expression darkened. "She had a coach who had come from Europe and was very highly recommended. He wasn't associated with the Olympic program, but everyone figured it wouldn't be long before he was. Diana was the envy of quite a few skaters for having secured his services. At any rate, the man was a first class cousin to Attila the Hun. He didn't know the meaning of the word rest or praise. He drove Diana nearly into the ground with extra hours of practice and even longer hours of constant viewing of her work with each little flaw a reason for screaming about her gracelessness. She took it all without a word. They were skating here at the time. I didn't like the man and neither did Maggie. One day, by accident, I overheard one of their training sessions. I was stunned at the way the man was behaving. I waited until practice was over to corner Diana and demand what was going on, and if all her meetings with him followed that pattern. It took a while, but she admitted they did. I asked her why she put up with it.''

"Let me guess, her family was paying a fortune for the great man, the pre-Olympic trials were in sight, and there was no gold without pain and sacrifice," Jason murmured bleakly.

"That's about it. I tried to tell her that the man was crazy. That there were really great coaches around who wouldn't work her to death. That his kind of training ultimately would destroy her. She wouldn't listen. The guy's reputation was too good. She stuck it out for six more months; she'd already been with him eighteen months. I watched her lose weight, grow so nervous that when you were around her it was honestly scary. Then one day, about two weeks before the trials were due to start, I found her in the changing room, out cold on the floor. Maggie and I took her to the emergency room. It turned out the doctor on staff there was a friend of one of the doctors who handled the physicals on the pre-Olympic skaters. He called his friend to check Diana's history. The other man was stunned to discover she was still skating. She had been diagnosed with what in layman's terms is called walking pneumonia. Her coach, the bastard, had been notified. He hadn't told Diana. How he expected to get her into the trials that way is beyond me. But he had deliberately risked her health, perhaps her life, with his actions."

"What did you do?"

"Called her parents and told them. Diana's father and I cornered the creep later at the rink and fixed his pretty face for him," he muttered, remembered rage making his voice rough.

"Why didn't any of this come out in the papers?"

"You know what a story like this would have done to the program. Plus, we also discovered the man was into heavy gambling and had run some bets through a second party on Diana losing. With her the favorite, which she would have been, he would have cleaned up. And besides, it definitely wasn't representative of the really great people involved in amateur sports. You've been there. You know. The committee came to Diana in the hospital, pleaded with her to leave out the details of what had happened. The coach was shuttled out of here so fast he was glad to keep his mouth shut just to avoid losing his freedom. Diana's father was talking about legal action at the time. All of us tried to talk Diana into coming out with the truth. We understood the committee's stand, but felt it wasn't fair to Diana. She wouldn't have any of it. She lay in that damn bed like a broken doll and promised no one would ever hear the real story from her, that she would protect the Olympics and those people who really made it work. I was never more furious in my life, nor more proud of her. I don't know that I could have taken a stand for an ideal and stuck with it the way she did. She took every bit of trash the press threw at her without a word in her own defense. But it cost her. I don't think any of us, even Diana, realized how much until she tried to go back to skating. It was as though all the horror of those two years had burned her ability to skate in front of an audience right out of her.''

He shook his head remembering. ''Her family, Maggie, and I had gathered for a little pre-show before she took up training again. Diana skated onto the ice, the music started, and she froze. I don't think I'll ever forget the look of horror in her eyes as long as I live. By the time we realized what was happening, she was shaking. Her father carried her off the ice and she hasn't been in front of more than one or two people she really trusts since.''

Jason cursed long and hard, his expression tortured. ''And now, because of me, she's backed into a corner where she'll have to skate or face something even worse than before.''

''That's it,'' Nick agreed grimly.

For one more moment, Jason allowed himself a vision of just what he would do to Frank when he finally caught up with him. Then, he raised his head to look Nick in the eye. "I will tell her what happened and why." There was no real choice. He had promised Diana honesty. He would keep his word, regardless of the cost.

"And?"

"She can decide."

"What do you mean decide? There is no decision. She has to skate."

"Like hell. If she doesn't want to skate, I won't be the one to make her and neither will anyone else. I'll take the flack this time. The press loves nailing me. I'll give them something really good, if that's what it takes."

Nicky stared, stunned at the harsh, bitter tone. There was no doubting the rock-hard determination in Jason's eyes. For the first time since he had met Jason, he began to see the man beneath the glacier look. It was that glimpse of the inner-being that made him change his mind about helping Jason find Diana. "She's at her parents' cabin in the woods." He pulled out a piece of paper and drew a sketchy but clear map. "This is the way to get there. It's not far, but it is isolated. She won't thank me for this, you know."

Jason took the paper, glanced at it, and then spoke, "But I do." He got to his feet. "I'm glad you and Maggie are her friends. If she won't let me help her, she'll need you all the more."

Diana walked up the trail slowly, her hands stuffed deep in her pockets, her eyes trained on the ground. Suddenly, she stiffened, her head lifted, her eyes widening at the sight of a car parked in front of the cabin. Jason. His car. She stopped in mid-stride. He was leaning against the hood, his ankles crossed, his arms folded across his chest, watching her. For a long moment, they stared at each other across the distance.

Finally, Diana could stand the silence no longer. She walked forward, knowing there was nowhere else to run even if she wanted to. "Why did you come?" she asked when she got even with him.

Jason studied her carefully blank face and knew that his position was worse than he had anticipated. He had never seen Diana so controlled, so empty of the fire he had come to associate with her. "To explain."

"Do you think you can?" Strangely, she felt nothing on seeing him beyond the shock of his appearance.

"If you'll let me."

"Why should I?"

Jason moved then, so quickly Diana had no time to evade his grasp. He caught her shoulders and drew her close to his body. "Oddly enough, I could say because of this, but I won't."

Diana couldn't deny the way her body softened despite her mental need to resist. "It's not enough," she retorted bluntly. "And if not this, then what?"

"Because you taught me that it isn't enough. Because I care what you think when I don't care what anyone else thinks, including Pippa and Lorelei. Because I don't want you hurt because of me, but I know damn well before this day is over you will be. Because I don't want you to find out what has happened from anyone but me. A hundred reasons, maybe. Those are just part of the list.'' The words poured out through his anger and frustration. ''Now, tell me to go. Tell me I wasted my time coming to find you. Tell me what we shared is over. That it was nothing.'' He dropped his hands, releasing her.

Diana felt something move beneath the layers of numbness. She would rather have kept the insulating cloak of neutrality, but Jason had ripped it from her with his confession. ''Damn you, you lied to me.'' Her temper erupted in spite of her best efforts to control it.

''I never have.''

''Then how did that sleaze get my number?''

''I don't know for sure because I haven't been able to get hold of him myself. Knowing Frank, I'd say he has some contact that owes him a favor, probably one of your clients.'' He pulled the poster that Nicky had given him out of his pocket. ''But that's not the worst of what he's done.'' He handed her the paper.

Diana gazed at him, unease turning to fear both at the look in his eyes and his tone. Slowly, she lowered her eyes as she unfolded the sheet. The sight of her name just below Jason's on the program stunned her. She blinked, praying that she was hallucinating and knowing that she wasn't.

With every muscle tense, Jason spoke slowly and distinctly, ''I didn't know about it. Nicky got it in the mail this morning and he was the last one on the list of places where it's been sent. Every major media contact in the country has one of these.''

''No!'' she breathed in horror, paling at the thought of performing again, of being judged, of all those eyes seeking a flaw in her routine. Helplessness washed over her. ''I can't do this. You'll have to call it back.''

Jason pulled her close, this time meeting no resistance as he sheltered her body with his strength. ''Is that what you really want, Diana?''

''Yes,'' she blurted without thinking. He was no longer the betrayer. He was the ally she needed, the shoulder to lean on to battle the storm that had all but destroyed her once.

Jason stared over her head into the silence of the forest. Every fiber of his being wanted to hold her close and protect her from the future that was plummeting down on them. He wanted to wipe out her past so she could step into the rink without fear. He wanted to silence the press and stand in an audience that would be as mesmerized by her skating as he was. He wanted to give her back the joy that must have been hers when she had won that first award. But he wasn't God. He couldn't work miracles on command. He was only a man. A man hurting for his woman, too tough to cry for her pain, but wishing he could if the tears would wash away the past. He felt a strange stirring in his heart. Suddenly, he knew what he had to do. What he had come to do was all wrong, for him, for

Diana, and for whatever the future might hold. Every nerve demanded he shelter and protect. But something stronger, something more clear-sighted demanded he take a terrible risk.

"I can't."

Diana raised her head, stunned at the finality of his tone. She stared at him. He met her look without flinching. "You mean you won't."

He felt as though his heart were being cut from his chest at her betrayed look. "All right, I won't."

She yanked herself out of his arms. "Damn you. Still the games. I believed you just now. Was I a fool?"

"This is no game." He stuffed his hands in his pockets to keep from shaking her or kissing her silent. Reaching her passion wouldn't work this time. He had to be calm. "You are the important issue here. Not the complex."

"I'll bet." She whirled from him, intent on escaping into the cabin. She half-expected him to stop her but he simply followed her retreat.

"Then you'd lose." He slammed the door behind him, shutting out the world and closing in on the problem. "You can't keep running. What happened to you back then was terrible. I'm glad that your father and Nicky beat the devil out of that sadist. But that doesn't mean that you can spend your life hiding. Aren't you the least bit curious, excited even? You wanted to be in front of an audience once. You loved it back then. You told me so. Do you want one twisted man to hold this kind of power over you for the rest of your life?''

For a fleeting instant, something inside Diana responded to the barrage of questions. ''You don't know what you're talking about. You walk out on the ice and forget people even exist. I'm not like that.''

''Neither am I any more. Don't you think I haven't felt the way my skating has changed since I met you? Don't you think that for the first time in my life I'm scared to step out into that rink? You've skated with me. You know what's going on. You know what happens to us when our style changes so dramatically. We need to be able to count on ourselves. I don't have that any more.''

Diana shook her head, fighting being affected by his words. She didn't want to feel sympathy for him. She didn't trust her strength to hold out against this kind of plea. ''You won't get me this way,'' she denied, wrapping her arms around herself.

''I'm not trying to get you. I want you to think, you crazy woman. I love you!'' he shouted. The words spilled out. He stopped as stunned by the declaration as she.

A week ago, she would have given her last breath to hear his words. ''You're lying.''

Jason shook his head. ''No. That more than anything tells me how little you value what we have shared. I have given you nothing but honesty almost from the first. I have tried to be open to you because I knew you needed it. I gave you things out of me that no one has had or ever will have. You feel betrayed. So do I. I trusted you, too, but you have believed me capable of doing something which I knew would hurt you badly. Even when you told me about your past, you left out the most important parts. You had to know I wouldn't have betrayed your trust, but you didn't give me that chance, did you? I had to find out the whole truth from Nicky. Still protecting yourself. Still holding back. You accuse me of being cold and I was. But are you any less in a different way? There are people out there, true lovers of figure skating, who would feel privileged to see you on ice, but you deny them and yourself that pleasure because one man used you so badly you almost lost yourself. You were a child then. You're a woman now, but you still think like a child.'' He reached into his pocket one final time and drew out a document. He handed it to her. "I brought you a gift. This one is something you'll need, and there isn't one string attached and no trick up my sleeves. Not that you'll believe that either, but as they say, the proof is in the pudding.''

Diana glanced down at the contract bearing her name.

"Read the last page when you get a chance. You might find it more interesting than you think.'' He slammed out of the cabin.

Diana made no move to stop him. She simply stood frozen, battered by words, emotions, and too many thoughts to sort through clearly. She heard the sound of Jason's car starting in the distance as though it were miles away. She didn't need to read the last page to know that somehow he was giving her her freedom.

Jason drove without thinking. Even now, he wasn't sure what had prompted him to take Diana's contract with him. He had meant to reason with her. He hadn't expected to slam into his own thoughts and discover just how clever he had been at fooling himself. Even now, he didn't know when or where he had fallen in love. He wasn't even comfortable with the emotion.

Shifting in his seat, he debated his course. He had to believe that Diana would see what she was doing to herself. That, too, felt strange. Love. A strange emotion. A bundle of doubts, stupid thoughts, and a trunkload of fear. He wanted her so much. She gave his life meaning and fire. She also brought confusion, frustration, and delight. She caught him on the raw with her anger, she drove him wild with her passion, and her skating was a dream on ice. She teased his mind and fulfilled his body. He loved her. He wasn't supposed to. He hadn't wanted to. But he did.

But did she love him? A question that logic didn't answer. Emotion only clouded and reason denied. Who knew? With this question, a very clear fear arose. Rejection. For the first time it mattered. Even now, he could feel the old walls closing in, strengthening, ready to protect him. He wanted to fight the need, but the old paths were safer than the new. What did a man do?

Diana stared at the phone, knowing she was a fool, knowing she was going to call a woman she barely knew, who seemed to be a friend and the holder of the key to Jason's mind. She picked up the receiver and dialed Pippa.

"I had a feeling you would be calling," Pippa murmured, on hearing Diana's voice.

"Then you knew more than I did," Diana mumbled, feeling awkward.

Pippa smiled. "I take it you have a problem."

"A large one."

"Tell me."

The comfortable, sympathetic tone was just the right note. Diana relaxed for the first time in days. Leaning back in the soft cushions on the couch, she let the words flow, leaving nothing out, no matter how small or trivial. Pippa listened without criticism, occasionally inserting a question or two, but for the most part being silent. When she was done, Diana felt drained, but curiously lighter.

"So, do you believe him?"

"I want to."

"That's an evasion."

Diana shifted restlessly. "All right. I do think he had nothing to do with this promotion or the agent's phone call."

"Well, that's a step in the right direction. Do you believe he loves you?"

Diana shied away from the question, then forced

herself to examine it. So many instances came to mind, moments when she had watched Jason struggle to express himself in clearly unfamiliar ways. A man who wanted an affair, no matter how fiery, didn't waste that kind of effort. But were his feelings real and lasting? Because of the man he was and the life he had led, maybe she was just a novelty and his love something so new and unfamiliar that he had mistaken its strength.

"Fiddle!" Pippa exclaimed.

Diana started at the snappy comment, not realizing that she had spoked aloud.

"My nephew is no fool, despite his past. Because he is so very unfamiliar with emotion, don't you think he would be even more leery of it and less likely to be mistaken?"

"Perhaps."

Pippa snorted rudely. "You know what I think? I think Jason was right. You are a coward. I wouldn't have thought it. He has the guts to be vulnerable, but you're running like a scared kid. Hell, I don't think you're good enough for my nephew."

Diana inhaled sharply at the thrust she hadn't been expecting. "That's not fair."

"Is any of this?" Pippa shot back. "Is what happened to you fair? What Frank did to you? To Jason? Think on that while you're playing with both your lives. Jason says he loves you. Believe him or don't, but make up your mind. For your sake and his." With that succinct advice, Pippa hung up.

Diana got to her feet, knowing that Pippa was right. She had needed the other woman's input to yank her up short. She was scared, but she knew what she had to do. There was one way to find out the truth.

TWELVE

Jason pulled on his skates and got to his feet. The rink was empty, just as it had been since the night Diana had left. The need to practice drove him onto the ice. He positioned his body for the opening move, waiting for the music to begin. He hadn't lied when he had told Diana how strange he felt with this new depth to his technique. It was almost impossible to judge whether the change was for the better. The melody opened in a explosion of sound. He erupted off his skates into a leap that demanded immediate attention and tremendous skill, without the momentum of forward motion to help in the liftoff. He settled back to the ice, his mind focused on his routine. It was a new one, something born in his mind as he had watched Diana practice night after night.

Diana stood in the shadows, stunned at the fury unleashed on the ice. She had never seen Jason skate so powerfully. He seemed at one with the frozen surface and the music. Her breath caught in her throat as he rose time after time into the air. Knowing the tremendous toll so many jumps took, she knew fear. He was alive with an intensity of feeling that was almost tangible. Moving without thought, she reached the rail, her hands gripping the smooth wood as the music reached its peak. A back somersault, beautifully performed, marked the spot. Intricate footwork carried Jason to the far end of the ice. He spun, twisted, and whirled away. Mesmerized, Diana followed every move, her breath coming in short pants between her parted lips. And then it was done. An abrupt ending that left her weak and wanting more.

Jason was breathing hard when he finished. He raised his head and saw Diana. Their eyes met. It was too much to hope she had come for him. It was enough that she had come at all. He glided slowly toward her, watching, waiting for some sign of why she was there. His love was too new, too unfamiliar to sit easily in his heart. He had risked a lot with his honesty. It was her turn now.

"It was wonderful," Diana whispered softly, searching his face. His eyes were clear and bright but unrevealing.

He shrugged, no more comfortable with his new style than he was with himself. "Strange. Different from my usual stuff."

Diana felt the wall between them and could have cried. Was Jason regretting his profession of love or was he guarding himself from her? "Better. More depth."

"Perhaps." He paused then asked, "Why did you come?"

Diana had hoped for a more open reception, but it was clear she wasn't going to get it. She pulled the contract from her handbag. It hadn't taken her long to realize that, while Jason could force her onto the ice, he had handed that weapon into her hands and left her to make her own decision. She had been stunned at the chance he was taking with his dream. He had every reason to believe she would leave him to face the press alone.

Diana took a short, deep breath, gathering her courage. There was so much between them. "To give you this. You were right. I have been running. I have stopped. I'll do the show."

Jason controlled the urge to drag her into his arms for a kiss that would probably burn them both alive. Fear held him back. He didn't want to lose her now. Until she showed that she wanted the same things he did, he had to give her room to come to terms with herself.

"I'm glad," he said simply.

Diana stared at him, stunned at the calm with which he received her news. "And that's all?" she demanded.

"What do you want me to say? I can't tell you I know it will be best for you because I'm not sure. Freezing in front of an audience is not something any performer ever forgets. I can't say I'm not glad for the complex's sake, because I am."

Diana collected her nerve. "And for you?"

Jason studied her for a moment, wondering if

that were really hope he saw in her eyes or just a trick of his own desperate need for some sign that she cared even a little for him. "I told you how I feel," he admitted finally, holding himself tense as he took another emotional risk.

Diana searched his face, wishing she dare believe him. "How can you be sure?"

He laughed harshly at the question. "It's odd, but I expected you to say that and hoped that you wouldn't. I thought I was the one who didn't trust, who held himself aloof. Lady, you have me beat by a mile. I have a better question for you. How do I prove that I love you? And better still, how do you prove that you love me, if you do?"

"I do!" she blurted, shocked that he didn't know. "I didn't want to and when I finally realized I couldn't fight you and myself any more, I started praying that you could feel even a little something for me."

Jason stared at her, unable to comprehend what he was hearing. His temper, ever on ready these days, slipped a notch. He controlled it, wanting to be certain he understood. "You mean to tell me that you have loved me all this time and not told me?" he demanded incredulously.

Diana took a step back at the bite of his tone. "How would I have told you without looking as though I were trying to get something from you?" she retaliated, the beginnings of anger in her voice.

Jason raked his fingers through his hair, reeling at the knowledge she had withheld. He felt cheated, betrayed. "All this time. I trusted you all this time and you withheld this kind of information. And you don't even see why I'm upset," he accused, glaring at her. "I thought I could count on you to give me the truth. You gave me your word. I turned myself inside out for you and you gave me lies by omission."

Diana was staggered at the charges and unable to refute them. Suddenly, her actions took on a new light. She lifted her hand to him, words of apology and love trembling on her lips. He backed from her, his skates hissing on the ice.

"No more." He shook his head. "I can't think. I came to Denver looking for a way to stop becoming a human machine. I watched you, when you competed and later through your routines. You had the passion I could never touch. I thought if I just got close to you for a while I could find my way back. Then I met you, wanted you until I couldn't see the reasons that brought me here. I gave what I had and discovered there was more. I trusted you as I have trusted no one."

"You're being unfair. We've both made mistakes," she protested, following him onto the ice. "What about your games?"

"Before I knew you. An old issue anyway, a smoke screen now." He looked down at the contract in his hands, his last trick, the defense he had given her gladly for the future he could not promise. "Why was it so very impossible to say I love you. I did it. The Iceman thawed at your feet and you let me do it without saying a word. Do you have any idea how much that hurts?" His smile was a study in self-mockery, a painful thing to see. "I wanted to feel again. I knew you could teach me. I just didn't expect this."

Diana grabbed his arms, trying but not succeeding in shaking him. "Listen to yourself," she pleaded fighting as she never had before for their love. "I love you. I couldn't tell you without making my emotions a burden and a prison for you. Think, Jason. What would you have done? What did you do when you gave me a way out of this show at the cost of your dream and your own feelings? I saw your face when you told me what I had become. It hurt you to say those words, but you did because you loved me. I did no less. I held secret something I wanted to shout to the world. I waited for some sign that you cared beyond the passion we shared. I paid a price for my silence. Was that a selfish act? A lie? A betrayal?" She was breathing hard when she finished—frightened, determined, and praying with every ounce of her strength.

Jason stared into her blazing eyes and read the truth. Relief unlocked his voice and his thoughts. "I've been a fool. I thought I controlled my life until I met you. I overreacted." He touched her face, tracing her lips as she smiled tenderly against his fingers. Her smile was a balm, a benediction. "I don't know how you can love me."

"I love you as you love me. Against all reason and all time. We belong together, both on and off the ice. And I'll prove it to you as you once challenged me to do.'' she said, an impulse turning into a certainty.

He bent his head, nuzzling her neck. Now that she had given him the assurance that he was loved, he didn't care what she asked of him. "How?"

Her laugh was rich, free, a woman's pleasure in her man and the tomorrow they had won. "Let's skate together. You know that each of us has to do one performance. We both need a solo out there to say good-by to our pasts. But what about hello to our future?"

"Do you mean it?" He lifted his head, pride adding a new dimension to this feeling called love. Her courage and freedom from the damage of the past were vivid in her expression. "You're sure?"

"Sure enough to do the asking.'' She hadn't known she could face an audience again without fear, hadn't known Jason's belief in her could touch the raw places in her soul.

"Yes." He gathered her close, his hands molding her body to his. "And now I have a question, light of my life. Will you marry me and be my love, share my bed and fortune and hold me when I need you and let me be there for you always, in all ways."

Diana looked into his eyes and saw what was in her heart reflected there. "Yes," she whispered. "I will share your life gladly and with all my heart."

"It's a lifetime commitment, I'm asking."

"I know."

"Starting today."

"This second." She smiled at the flash of desire in his eyes. "Right here, if I didn't like my privacy."

He grinned, suddenly very glad he had let that fool decorator he hired talk him into a massive couch in his new office. "Honey, have I got something to show you," he whispered as he urged her off the ice.

Diana giggled, feeling incredibly young and carefree. "I'll just bet," she teased as he sat down and yanked off his skates.

He gave her a pained look just before he pulled her into his lap and took her lips with a hard, deep kiss. "Behave, woman, or I won't let you play in my new office. Specifically, on one very long, overstuffed couch behind a sturdy, locked door with the phone off the hook."

He rose, lifting her as she looped her arms around his neck. "I do like the way you think, my love," she murmured, nipping at his neck as he headed down the hall. She had a vague glimpse of Nicky with Maggie behind him in the door to his own office. Their pleased smiles were an added but unnecessary bonus. As long as she had Jason, she had everything she needed.

Jason entered his suite, kicking the door shut behind him. He set Diana on her feet, his eyes holding hers. "I was so afraid I had lost you." He could admit it now that he had her.

"And I you. But never again. We found each other and that's all that matters."

* * *

Jason stood next to Diana as they watched the second to the last performance. The crowd for the benefit was larger than anticipated, standing room only. The last few weeks had been hectic, the press hounding both Diana and him about the details of the complex and Diana's return to the limelight. None of it had been easy and all of it had been draining both on their physical energies and their time together.

He glanced at Diana, noting the concentration that she was giving to the man on the ice. As always, he felt a warmth build inside at the passion that lurked in her eyes. Not passion for lovemaking, although that always seemed to be present when she looked at him, but passion for life. Every day with her was a revelation. He found pleasure in the strangest things and contentment in silence. Slipping his arm around her shoulders, he hugged her close.

"Nervous, darling?"

Diana leaned her head on Jason's shoulder, at peace with herself. "No."

He dropped a kiss on the top of her head. "I'm glad."

She glanced up at him with a smile that held equal parts of mischief and knowledge. "It's all that practicing we did."

His eyes gleamed with laughter, though not one hint of amusement appeared in his expression. "You liked that, did you?"

She laughed softly as the music came to a stop. "I wasn't the only one." The applause made speaking difficult, but neither needed words. Now there was silence. The announcer made Diana's introduction. The audience went wild. Her time had come.

"Burn up the ice, my love."

She tossed her head, her smile flashing with confidence and love. "Then you'll only have a puddle on which to skate," she teased before gliding onto the frozen surface.

Immediately the crowd silenced. The lights dimmed, leaving only a spotlight on Diana's poised figure. Then there was sound—a soft, eerie melody played on a pan flute. A graceful twirl, hands lifted, moving in a human imitation of wings. A glide on blades cutting patterns of deep edges and intense control in the ice. The first leap. A study in flash, brilliance, and delicacy as Diana floated back to earth, the woman counterpart of the bird she portrayed.

Jason watched, his breath keeping time with hers. His muscles flexed and tightened again and again with each jump. Diana was magic on ice. He watched, stunned by the power and beauty she unleashed. He had seen her skate many times, but never like this. The audience, too, must have sensed the extraordinary happening. No one moved, no sound was heard beyond the music and the woman who flew over and above the frozen arena. Jason leaned forward, his gaze concentrating on her. His love and desire for her perfection poured out. She turned, her eyes finding his as she stepped into the air for her final and most difficult lift. He held his breath for her height was far greater than was safe and yet when she landed it was almost as though she had never left the ground, so smooth was her return. The crowd went wild, the applause drowning out the last strains of the flute. The lights died, but the praise went on and on.

The lights came on again and Diana stood in the center of the ring accepting the tribute that had ceased to matter. She turned from her audience to the man she loved. The flowers thrown from the watchers littered the ice. She skated to one lone orchid, lifted it to her lips as Jason glided into the rink in response to the announcer's introduction. As they passed, his hand reached for hers. She dropped the orchid in his palm. He smiled and raised it to his lips before tucking it into the lapel of his costume.

Diana took his place on the sidelines. Forever after the skating world would remember one brief shining moment when two stars, one shrouded in mystery and one wrapped in cold brilliance, had burned up the ice with their passion. Jason's reception after his performance was no less dramatic and overwhelming than Diana's. When the audience demanded an encore, the announcer came on to add two surprises to an evening already filled to overflowing with them. Diana and Jason would skate together and later in the month would make the partnership on ice one in real life with a marriage.

Jason stood in the center of the ring, amid the calls for more and held out his hand. Diana, her eyes only on him, glided onto the ice. Her orchid still fluttered against his heart. She smiled as she took her place in the circle of his arms and waited for the music to begin one final time.

"You should have warned me about a public announcement," she whispered in the darkness.

"And spoil the moment. Never, my love." He kissed her quickly, an instant before the lights went up and their first public duo began.

The reporters were stunned, the skating world amazed. The Iceman had melted. Their pair skating had been elegant lovemaking on ice. No woman had left the rink with a dry eye and no man had watched the two of them without envying Jason his Diana.